CRITICS CHEER
JULIE GARWOOD'S
FOR THE ROSES

"Ms. Garwood combines the Old West and England to create an incredibly entrancing tale with a cast of unique characters that will certainly linger in your heart. Her gifted prose is always a treat, and *FOR THE ROSES* is no exception."

—*Rendezvous*

"An enchanting tale with a happy ending . . ."
—*Abilene Reporter-News*

"A powerful story about four urchin boys who rescue a baby in New York City, it's filled with characters you'll never forget."

—*Romantic Reader News*

"Lively and charming . . . Filled with humor and appealing characters . . ."

—*Library Journal*

"[A] page-turner filled with lots of family values . . . the reader is never out of Garwood's skillful comfort zone."
—*Kirkus Reviews*

"As wild as the Old West . . . "

—*Publishers Weekly*

"There will be moments when you'll laugh and cry, and others when the warmth and love captured here will enfold you in its powerful embrace. With a master's pen, Julie Garwood explores the heart and soul of a family whose love and loyalty will truly inspire. *FOR THE ROSES* is a brilliant achievement."

—*Romantic Times*

Books by Julie Garwood

Gentle Warrior
Rebellious Desire
Honor's Splendour
The Lion's Lady
The Bride
Guardian Angel
The Gift
The Prize
The Secret
Castles
Saving Grace
Prince Charming
For the Roses
The Wedding
One Pink Rose

Published by POCKET BOOKS

JULIE GARWOOD

One Pink Rose

POCKET BOOKS

New York London Toronto Sydney Tokyo Singapore

This book is a work of fiction. Names, characters, places and incidents are products of the author's imagination or are used fictitiously. Any resemblance to actual events or locales or persons, living or dead, is entirely coincidental.

An *Original* Publication of POCKET BOOKS

POCKET BOOKS, a division of Simon & Schuster Inc.
1230 Avenue of the Americas, New York, NY 10020

ISBN: 0-671-01008-5

First Pocket Books printing June 1997

10 9 8 7 6 5 4 3 2 1

POCKET and colophon are registered trademarks of Simon & Schuster Inc.

Printed in the U.S.A.

One
Pink
Rose

Prologue

❧

*L*ong ago there lived a remarkable family. They were the Claybornes, and they were held together by bonds far stronger than blood.

They met when they were boys living on the streets in New York City. Runaway slave Adam, pickpocket Douglas, gunslinger Cole, and con man Travis survived by protecting one another from the older gangs roaming the city. When they found an abandoned baby girl in their alley, they vowed to make a better life for her and headed west.

They eventually settled on a piece of land they named Rosehill, deep in the heart of Montana Territory.

The only guidance they received as they were growing up came from the letters of Adam's mother,

Rose. Rose learned about her son's companions from their heartfelt letters to her, for they confided their fears, their hopes and their dreams, and in return she gave them what they had never had before, a mother's unconditional love and acceptance.

In time, each came to know her as his own Mama Rose.

After twenty long years, Rose joined them. Her sons and daughter were finally content. Her arrival was, indeed, a cause for both celebration and consternation. Her daughter was married to a fine man and expecting her first child, and her sons had grown to be honorable, strong men, each successful in his own right. But Mama Rose wasn't quite satisfied just yet. They had become too settled in their bachelor ways to suit her. Since she believed God helps those who help themselves, there was only one thing left for her to do.

She was going to meddle.

Time of Roses

It was not in the Winter
Our loving lot was cast;
It was the time of roses—
We pluck'd them as we pass'd!

—Thomas Hood (1798–1845)

One

❧

Rosehill Ranch, Montana Valley, 1880

Travis Clayborne was thinking hard about killing a man.

The youngest brother had only just returned home from the southern tip of the territory and planned to stay one night before he resumed his hunt. Thus far, his prey had managed to stay a step ahead of him. He had thought he had him good and trapped near the gorge, but then the elusive devil had vanished into thin air. Travis grudgingly admitted he would have to tip his hat to this stranger who had outwitted him. He might also have to compliment him on his survival skills. Then he'd shoot him.

He'd taken to the notion of doing in the culprit right away. The enemy's name was Daniel Ryan, and the sin he'd committed wasn't forgivable by a son's measure. Ryan had dared to take advantage of a sweet, innocent, genteel old lady with a heart of gold—Travis's own Mama Rose to be exact—and in Travis's heart and mind, killing him was almost too good for him. Now Travis was trying to convince himself that justice would be on his side.

That evening he waited until their mother had gone to bed to discuss the atrocity with his brothers. They sat side by side on the porch with their booted feet propped up on the railing, their heads tilted back, and their eyes closed.

Harrison, their brother-in-law, joined them a moment after Rose went upstairs. He thought the brothers looked content and was about to tell them so when Travis declared his intentions. Harrison sat down hard in the chair next to Douglas, stretched his long legs out, and then begged to differ with Travis. He said that the law should take care of the thief, and that this person, like every other man and woman in this fair country, was entitled to a trial. If he was proven guilty, he would be sent to prison for his punishment. He shouldn't be murdered in cold blood.

None of the Claybornes paid any attention to Harrison's pontificating. He was an attorney by trade, and it was in his nature to argue about every little thing. All of the brothers thought it was kind of sweet the way Harrison believed in justice for everyone. Their little sister's husband was a decent man, but he was from Scotland and, in their minds, naive about the laws in the wilderness. Perhaps in a perfect world the innocent would always be protected and the guilty would always be punished, but they didn't happen to live in a perfect world, now did they? They lived in Montana Territory.

Besides, what lawman in his right mind would take the time and trouble to hunt down a garden snake when there were so many deadly rattlers out there just waiting to strike?

Harrison refused to bend to the Clayborne way of looking at things. He was appalled by Travis's decision to go after the culprit who had robbed their mother; he reminded Travis that he had a duty as a future attorney to behave with honor. He also suggested Travis reread Plato's *Republic*.

Travis wouldn't be deterred from what he proclaimed was a sacred mission. He leaned forward to look at Harrison when he gave his argument.

"A son's first duty is to his mother," he declared.

"Amen," Douglas muttered.

"It's clear to all of us that Mama Rose was duped," Travis continued. "He asked to see the gold case and the compass, didn't he?"

"I wish she hadn't told him about it," Adam interjected.

"But she did tell him," Douglas said. "And I'm guessing as soon as she mentioned it was gold, that's when he asked to see it."

"He knew he was going to steal it then," Cole said.

"It was clever of him to let the crowd separate them," Adam said.

"Mama Rose told us this Ryan fellow is well over six feet tall. He's bulky too," Douglas reminded them. "Bulky probably means he's got more muscle than most. Seems peculiar to all of us such a big man could be pushed around by a crowd. He meant to steal it, all right."

"For God's sake, Douglas, you cannot assume—" Harrison began.

Travis cut him off. "No one takes advantage of our mama and gets away with it. It's up to one of her sons to right this wrong. Surely you can understand how we feel, Harrison. You had a mother once, didn't you?"

"I wouldn't bet on it," Cole drawled out, just to get Harrison riled up.

His brother-in-law wasn't in the mood to take exception to the remark. "Your reasoning is twisted," he said. He waited until the derisive snorting had stopped before he announced that Travis's plan to shoot the thief was premeditated murder.

Cole laughed at Harrison, reached around Douglas to slap him on his back for saying something so amusing, and then suggested Harrison start thinking about a way to get Travis released from jail should he be arrested for doing a son's duty. He also suggested Travis simply drag the culprit back to Montana and let all the brothers shoot him.

Harrison was nearly ready to admit defeat. It was impossible to talk sense into any of the brothers. The only thing that was keeping him sane was the fact that deep in his heart he knew none of them would ever commit cold-blooded murder. They sure enjoyed talking about it though.

"How do you know the man you're after is really Daniel Ryan? He could have made up the name," he remarked. "He could also have lied about being from Texas."

"Nope," Cole said. "He told Mama Rose his name and where he was from before she started talking about the presents she was bringing to us."

"Thank God she didn't tell him about the other gifts. He probably would have stolen my pocket watch," Douglas said.

"I'll bet he would have taken my map too," Adam interjected.

"And my leather-bound books," Travis added.

"The thief's from Texas, all right," Adam said. "He had a peculiar drawl in his speech."

"That's right," Douglas remembered. "She thought it was . . . What'd she call it, Travis?"

"Charming," he replied with a frown.

"Never did like the names Daniel or Ryan," Cole announced. "Come to think of it, I don't have much use for Texans either. Can't trust them."

Harrison rolled his eyes heavenward. "You never did like anyone or anything," he reminded him. "Do me a favor and don't say another word until I go upstairs. You're making me forget I'm a logical man."

Cole laughed. "You're the one who insisted on moving back into Rosehill with your wife. I'm part of Rosehill, Harrison, like it or not."

"Mary Rose needs to be with her mother during her confinement. I'm not about to go from town to town with Judge Burns and leave her alone in Blue Belle. And by the way, the next time you tell her she waddles like a duck, I'm going to punch you. Got that? She's a little emotional right now and doesn't need to be told she's as big as a—"

Cole wouldn't let him finish. "All right, we'll stop teasing her. She sure is getting pretty, isn't she?"

"She was always pretty," Adam said.

"Yes, but now that she's carrying my nephew, she's even prettier. Don't you dare tell her what I just admitted, or she'll never let me live it down. My sister likes to torment me whenever she can, and frankly, I can't imagine why."

He noticed the gleam that came into Harrison's eyes and knew the man was about to say something to provoke him. Since Cole wasn't in the mood to argue tonight, he decided to turn the topic back to the more pressing business at hand, catching a low-down, thieving garden snake who had slithered all the way up to Montana Territory from Texas.

"Travis, are you going to leave tomorrow?"

"Yes."

"How was it decided you would be the one to go after Daniel Ryan?" Harrison asked. "If the Texan really did steal your brother's compass, and I'm only willing to concede that the possibility exists, then shouldn't Cole be the one to go after him? The compass was meant for him."

"Cole can't go anywhere just yet," Adam explained.

"He was to lay low until old Shamus Harrington calms down," Douglas added.

"What did you do, Cole?" Harrison asked, already dreading the answer.

"He defended himself," Adam said. "One of Harrington's sons thought he was faster with his gun than Cole and forced a shoot-out."

"What happened?" Harrison asked.

"I won," Cole said with a grin.

"Obviously," Harrison snapped. "Did you kill him?"

"No, but almost," he admitted. "It was really kind of strange the way he came after me," he added. "Lester had fallen in with a gang passing through Blue Belle, and the word on the street was that they were planning to rob the bank in Hammond, Saturday next," he added.

"Does seem odd he'd come after you," Douglas agreed. "Lester's been strutting around acting like a big man in front of his new friends. Maybe he wanted to impress them."

"I heard they goaded him into the shoot-out with you," Adam said. "Dooley told me they acted like they knew who you were, Cole."

"Dooley's been hanging around his friend Ghost too long," Cole said. "You can't take anything either one of them says as fact, Adam."

"They probably heard of your reputation," Douglas suggested.

"They were just looking for trouble," Cole said. "Besides, everyone knows Harrington's sons are as dumb as dirt."

"True, but old man Shamus is still going to hold a grudge," Douglas said. "Mountain men do when one of their own gets shot, and since he has five other sons, you're going to have to be real careful for a long time."

"I'm always careful," Cole boasted. "Now that I think about it, I could go after Ryan, Travis. You've got enough to do without—"

His brother wouldn't let him finish. "No, you're staying here," he said. "Besides, I've got everything all planned out."

"That's right," Douglas said. "He's going to kill three birds with one stone."

Travis nodded. "I'm going to take my papers to Wellington and Smith so everything will be in order when I begin my apprenticeship with their law firm in September, and since Hammond's just a jump away from Pritchard, I'll take care of that business Mama Rose stuck me with, then swing on over to River's Bend, shoot Ryan, pick up the birthday present back in Hammond, and come back here in time for the celebration."

"You owe us ten dollars for Mama Rose's birthday gift," Cole reminded Harrison.

"What are we getting her?" he asked.

"A fancy sewing machine," Douglas said. "Her eyes lit up when she saw a picture of it in the catalog Adam gave her. We're getting her the most expensive model, of course. She deserves the best."

Harrison nodded. "Aren't Golden Crest and River's Bend in opposite directions?"

"Just about," Cole said. "Which is why I think I should go after Ryan, Travis. It would save you—"

Once again his brother wouldn't let him finish. "You've got to lay low," he said.

Harrison agreed and offered an alternative that would save Travis time and trouble.

"Surely you can get a sewing machine in Pritchard and save yourself several days' riding."

"I suppose he could," Cole said. "But Ryan wasn't spotted in Pritchard. He was headed for River's Bend yesterday."

"And how would you know that?" Harrison asked.

"We put the word out to let us know if anyone runs

into him," Adam said. "Travis, it's a pity you have to do that favor first. By the time you reach River's Bend, Ryan will probably be long gone."

"I've got it all figured out," Travis said. "It should only take a day of hard riding to deliver this Emily Finnegan woman to her groom in Golden Crest, and if it's dry enough, I can cut through the gully and be in River's Bend the following afternoon."

"You're dreaming," Adam told him. "It's been raining off and on for a month now. That gully's going to be filled. Why, it will take you at least three days to go around."

"Who is Emily Finnegan?" Harrison asked.

"She's the favor I'm doing for Mama Rose," Travis said.

Harrison gritted his teeth. Getting information out of the brothers was an arduous undertaking, but he was tenacious enough to persevere. The Claybornes liked to confuse him with spurious facts, none of which were the least bit relevant. They did it on purpose, of course. They were united in their goal to make him stop "hounding" them, as Cole would say, which meant they didn't want him to question either their motives or their ethics. Three of the brothers still believed they could "out stubborn" him. Adam was the only one who knew better. No one was as stubborn as a Scotsman, and since Harrison had been born and raised in the Highlands, he qualified.

"What's the favor?" he asked Travis again.

"Mama Rose had supper with the Cohens last week, and they happened to tell her about a woman who was stuck in Pritchard. Her escort up and died on her, and she's been trying to get someone to take her on to Golden Crest, but hasn't had any success."

"Why doesn't the man she's going to marry ride down to Pritchard and get her?"

"I asked Mama Rose that very question, and she told me it wouldn't be proper. The preacher's waiting in Golden Crest, and it's up to Miss Emily Finnegan to get there on her own. Mama Rose offered my services."

"She must have thought Hammond was right next door to Golden Crest," Douglas said.

"Why can't someone from Pritchard escort her?" Harrison asked. "It's a good-sized town. Surely she can find some willing couple there."

"People are mighty superstitious in Pritchard," Cole said.

"What does that mean?" Harrison asked.

"It means Miss Emily spooks them," he explained.

"It seems poor Miss Emily has gone through quite a few escorts," Douglas said.

"How many?" Harrison wanted to know.

"Too many to keep track of," Cole answered, deliberately exaggerating. "Rumor has it a couple of them died. Travis, you'd better take something with you for luck," he added with a nod in his brother's direction. "I'd give you my lucky compass, but then I don't have it, now do I, and all because that sneaking, no good son of a—"

Harrison cut him off before he could get riled up again. "You can't know if the compass will bring you luck or not, Cole. You've never seen the thing."

"Mama Rose chose it for me, didn't she? That makes it lucky."

"You're as superstitious as the folks in Pritchard," he muttered. "Travis, do you think you'll have trouble with this Miss Emily?"

"No," he answered. "I'm not superstitious, and I don't believe half of what they're saying about her either. How bad can she be?"

Two

❧

The woman was a walking plague.

They hadn't even gotten out of town before Travis was punched, kicked, tripped, and shot at, but not by anyone from Pritchard. No, it was Miss Emily Finnegan who tried to do him in, and even though she swore on her sainted mother's grave that it had all been a terrible misunderstanding, Travis didn't believe her. Why would he? He had it on good authority from his friends the Cohens that Miss Emily's mother was still alive and probably dancing an Irish jig with Mr. Finnegan back in Boston, now that the two of them had unloaded their ungrateful daughter on a poor, unsuspecting stranger living in Golden Crest.

Admittedly, Miss Emily was a pretty little thing. She had hair the color of sable that curled softly around her ears, and big hazel eyes that were brown one minute and gold the next. She had a real nice mouth too, until she opened it, which, Travis was quick to notice, was most of the time. The woman had an opinion about everything and felt compelled to share it with him so that there wouldn't be any future misunderstandings.

She wasn't a know-it-all, but she sure came close. He formed his opinion just five painful minutes after he'd met her.

It had been suggested by Olsen, the hotel proprietor, that they meet in front of the stage coach station. Travis spotted her from way down the street. She was standing directly behind the hitching post, holding a black umbrella in one hand and a pair of white gloves in the other. There were at least six satchels lined up in a neat row in front of her on the boardwalk, entirely too many to drag up the side of a mountain.

Miss Finnegan was dressed to perfection from head to toe in white linen. He assumed she hadn't had time to change out of her Sunday best church clothes. Then he remembered it was Thursday.

They didn't exactly start out on the right foot. She was standing at attention with her shoulders back and her head held high, watching the commotion across the street. Although it was still early in the morning, a rowdy crowd had already gathered in Lou's Tavern and were making quite a ruckus. Perhaps that was why she didn't hear him come up behind her.

He made the mistake of tapping her lightly on her shoulder to get her attention so that he could tip his hat to her and introduce himself. That's when she shot at him. It happened so fast, he barely had enough time to get out of the way. The little derringer she had concealed under her gloves went off when she whirled around. The bullet would have gotten him smack in his middle if he hadn't spotted the gleaming barrel and leapt to the side in the nick of time.

He was pretty certain the gun housed only one chamber, but he wasn't taking any chances. In a flash, he grabbed hold of her wrist and twisted her arm up so that her weapon was aimed toward the sky. Only then did he move close so he could give her a piece of his mind.

And that's when she whacked him with her umbrella and kicked him hard in his left kneecap. It was apparent that she was aiming for his groin, and when she missed her mark the first time, she had the gall to try again.

He made up his mind then that Miss Emily Finnegan was crazy.

"Unhand me, you miscreant."

"Miscreant? What in thunder's a miscreant?"

She didn't have the faintest idea. She was so taken aback by the question she almost shrugged in response. Granted, she didn't know what a "miscreant" was, but she did know that her sister, Barbara, used the word whenever she wanted to discourage an overzealous admirer, and it had always been very effective. What worked for her conniving sister was going to start working for her. Emily had made that vow on the train from Boston.

"You only need to know that it's an insult," she said. "Now, let go of me."

"I'll let go of you after you promise to stop trying to kill me. I'm your escort to Golden Crest," he added with a scowl. "Or was, until you shot at me. You're going to have to get up there on your own now, lady, and if you kick me one more time, I swear I'll—"

She interrupted him before he could tell her he'd toss her in the water trough.

"You're Mr. Clayborne? You can't be," she stammered out, a look of horror on her face. "You aren't . . . an old man."

"I'm not young either," he snapped. "I am Travis Clayborne," he added, but because his knee was still throbbing from being kicked by the bit of fluff, he didn't bother to tip his hat to her. "Give me your gun."

She didn't argue. She simply placed the weapon in the palm of his hand and frowned up at him. She didn't apologize either. He noticed that slight right away.

"I swear I'm going to be limping for a week. What have you got in your shoes? Iron?"

Her smile was dazzling, and heaven help him for noticing, she had a cute little dimple in her right cheek. If he hadn't already decided he didn't like her, he would have thought she was a might better than simply pretty. She was downright lovely. He had to remind himself the crazy woman had just tried to kill him.

"What a silly thing to suggest," she said. "Of course I don't have iron in my shoes. I'm sorry I kicked you, but you did sneak up on me."

"I did no such thing."

"If you say so," she said, trying to placate him. "You were teasing me about changing your mind, weren't you? You wouldn't really abandon a helpless lady in her hour of need, would you?"

The little woman had a sense of humor. Travis jumped to that conclusion as soon as she told him she was helpless. She'd said it with a straight face too, and, honest to Pete, it didn't matter that his shin was still stinging from her wallop of a kick; he still felt like laughing. He couldn't wait to be rid of her, of course, but he was in a much better frame of mind.

Mr. Clayborne was taking entirely too long to answer her question. The thought of once again being stranded in the middle of nowhere sent chills down her spine. She let out a little sigh and decided there was only one thing to do.

God help her, she was going to have to flirt with the scoundrel. With a little sigh she pulled out the useless little pink-and-white painted fan she'd purchased in St. Louis for entirely too much money, flipped it open with the dainty turn of her wrist she'd practiced for hours on the train, and held it in front of her face. She was deliberately concealing her cheeks so he wouldn't see her blush of embarrassment when she did something she considered utterly ridiculous.

She wasn't just going to try to flirt; she was also going to be coy. She drew a quick breath to keep herself from groaning, then batted her eyelashes up at him in imitation of her sister's tactics. Barbara had always looked very coy; Emily was pretty certain *she* looked like an idiot. God only knew, she felt like one.

She realized her practical, down-to-earth nature was trying to reassert itself and immediately tried to squelch it. She had vowed to change everything about herself, and she wasn't about to give up now, no matter how foolish she felt.

Travis watched her flutter her eyelashes at him for a

long silent minute. No doubt about it, she was crazy all right, and he suddenly felt a little sorry for her. She was definitely out of her element, dressed as she was for a Sunday social in the center of the dirt and grime known as Pritchard, trying her best to be painfully correct in her manners.

He knew she was trying to manipulate him now and decided to have a bit of sport with her.

"Maybe you ought to see Doc Morganstern before you go anywhere, ma'am. He might have something to help stop your eyes from twitching. I don't mean to be indelicate, but it's got to be bothering you."

She slapped her fan closed and let out a loud sigh. "You're either as completely thickheaded as a tree, Mr. Clayborne, or I still haven't perfected it yet."

"Perfected what?" he asked.

"Flirting, Mr. Clayborne. I was trying to flirt with you."

Her honesty impressed him. "Why?"

"Why? So that you would do what I want you to do, of course. I'm not much good at it though, am I?"

He didn't answer the absurd question. "The twitching's stopped," he drawled out, just to get her dander up.

"I wasn't twitching," she muttered. "There isn't anything wrong with my eyes, thank you very much. I was simply practicing my technique on you, that's all. Shall we go and collect Mrs. Clayborne and be on our way? I do hope she's more pleasant than you are, sir. Please stop gawking at me. I want to reach my destination before dark."

"There isn't any Mrs. Clayborne."

"Oh, that won't do."

He leaned down close to her. "Will you please say something that makes sense?"

She took a step away from him. The man was entirely too good-looking for her sensibilities. He had the most wonderful green eyes. She'd noticed the color while he was growling at her with obvious irritation and asking her such rude questions. She'd noticed what a masculine, fit fellow he was too.

Travis Clayborne was tall, on the thin side, but with muscles galore on his shoulders and arms. She didn't dare look any lower, or he'd get the notion she was going to try to kick him again, but she was certain his legs were just as well-endowed.

No doubt about it, he was an extremely handsome man. Women probably chased after him all the time. Foolish females would be helpless against those beautiful green eyes of his. His smile could cause considerable havoc too. Why, he'd just smiled at her once and for the barest of seconds, but it was still quite enough to make her heartbeat quicken. He probably had broken hundreds of women's hearts already, and she wasn't about to be added to his list. She had already learned that painful lesson, thank you very much.

Miss Finnegan was suddenly glaring up at him, and he couldn't figure out what had caused the sudden change. "I asked you why I have to be married to escort you to Golden Crest."

"Because it wouldn't be at all proper for me to go riding into the wilderness with such a handsome man. What will people think?"

"Who cares what people think? You don't know anyone here, do you?"

"No, but I will get to know them, once I'm married to Mr. O'Toole. If Golden Crest is just a day's ride away, I'll probably be doing some of my shopping here. Surely you can understand my reservations, sir. I must keep up appearances."

He shrugged. "If you can't go with me, then I've fulfilled my promise to offer my services. Good day, ma'am."

He tried to walk away. She was clearly appalled by his behavior. "Wait," she called out, chasing after him. "You wouldn't leave me alone, would you? A gentleman would never abandon a lady in distress. . . ."

"I guess I'm not a gentleman," he told her without pausing in his long-legged stride down the walkway. "And I'm certain you aren't a lady in distress."

She grabbed hold of his arm, dug her heels in to stop him from taking another step, and found herself being dragged along in his wake.

"I most certainly am in distress, and it's vile of you to contradict me."

"I was handsome a minute ago, but now I'm vile?"

"You can be both," she told him.

He suddenly turned around to look at her. He knew he couldn't leave her stranded in Pritchard, not if he ever wanted to look his Mama Rose in the eyes again, and so he decided that the only way he was ever going to maintain his sanity while he led the woman to Golden Crest was to strike some sort of a bargain with her.

"I wouldn't consider it a compliment," she announced with a blush he had to admit was downright attractive.

"Consider what a compliment?"

"Being handsome. I thought Randolph Smythe was handsome too, and he turned out to be a hideous creature."

Don't ask, he told himself.

"Don't you want to know who Randolph Smythe is?"

"No, I don't want to know."

She told him anyway. "He's the man I was supposed to marry."

She went and pricked his interest with that statement. "But you didn't," he said.

"No, I didn't. I was ready to though."

"How ready?"

Her blush intensified. "Are you going to escort me to Golden Crest or not?"

He wouldn't let her change the subject now that it had gotten downright interesting.

"How ready?" he asked again.

"I waited at the altar for him. He didn't show up," she added with a quick nod.

"He jilted you? Well now, that was a real mean-spirited thing to do," he said in an attempt at kindness. "I can't imagine why he'd change his mind at the last minute."

He wasn't telling her the truth. He was pretty certain he knew exactly why good old Randolph had changed his mind. The man had come to his senses. Travis wondered if Emily had ever tried to shoot him. That would have been enough to send any man with half a mind running in the opposite direction.

"So there wasn't any wedding," he remarked for

lack of anything better to say. She was staring up at him with such an earnest, hopeful look on her face, and he guessed she expected him to say something a bit more sympathetic.

He gave it his best shot. "Some men just don't cotton to the notion of being tied down to one woman. Randolph was probably like that."

"No, he wasn't."

"Look, lady, I'm trying to be nice about it."

"Don't you want to know why he didn't show up at the church?"

"You shot at him, didn't you?"

"I did no such thing."

"I really don't want to know his reasons. All right? Suffice it to say, there wasn't any wedding."

"Oh, there was a wedding all right. Did I mention my sister didn't show up at the church either, Mr. Clayborne?"

"You're joking."

"I'm perfectly serious."

"Your sister and Randolph . . ."

"Are now legally married."

He was appalled. "What kind of family do you come from? Your own sister betrayed you?"

"We were never close," she assured him.

He squinted down at her. "I can't help but notice you don't appear to be overly distraught about it all."

Travis shook his head. He couldn't understand why the story intrigued him so. He didn't even know Randolph Smythe, yet he still felt like punching him in the nose for doing such a cruel thing to Emily. Come to think of it, he didn't know Emily Finnegan either. Why in thunder did he care?

She saw the pity in his eyes and promptly glared at him. "Don't you dare feel sorry for me, Mr. Clayborne."

She looked as though she wanted to kick him again. Any sympathy he felt for her vanished in a heartbeat.

"It was probably your own fault."

If looks could kill, they'd have been measuring him for a coffin now. Travis didn't back down after making his statement, but added a nod to let her know he meant what he'd said.

"And how is that?" she asked, and then accidentally whacked him with her umbrella when she folded her arms across her chest. Because he'd just made such a rude comment to her, she didn't apologize.

He thought she'd done it on purpose. He grabbed the umbrella, tossed it on top of her satchels, and then answered her.

"You chose an unfit, unscrupulous man; that's why it's your own fault, and you should realize by now that you're better off without him."

He had just redeemed himself in her eyes. He wasn't being cruel when he blamed her; he was only being honest. He was right too. She had chosen an unscrupulous man.

"Are you going to take me to Golden Crest or not?"

"What happened to the couple who was escorting you?"

"Be more specific, please."

"More specific?"

"Which couple are you referring to?" she asked. She got his full attention. "How many were there?"

"Three."

"Three people or three couples?"

"Couples," she answered.

He noticed she quickly lowered her gaze to the ground and looked uncomfortable. The topic was obviously a sore one. Then he remembered that his brother Cole had told him how the superstitious folks in Pritchard were spooked by Miss Emily Finnegan. He really should have paid more attention to the conversation, he decided, realizing that it was a little late to be worrying about it now. Still, he should get all the particulars before he took the woman anywhere, just to be on the safe side.

"You went through six escorts?"

"It was a very long trip, Mr. Clayborne."

"What happened to the first couple?"

"The Johnsons?"

"All right, the Johnsons," he agreed to get her to continue. "What happened to them?"

"It was really quite tragic."

He had had a feeling she was going to say that. "I bet it was. What'd you do to them?"

Her spine stiffened. "I didn't do anything to them. They became ill on the train, and I believe it was something they ate that made them sick. Quite a few of the other passengers became ill too," she added. "The Johnsons stayed in Chicago. I'm sure they're fully recovered by now."

"What happened to the second couple?"

"Do you mean the Porters? It was also quite tragic," she admitted. "They also became ill. The fish, you see."

"The fish?"

"Yes, they ate the fish too. I believe it had gone bad, and I did warn Mr. Porter, but he wouldn't listen to reason. He ate it anyway."

"And?"

"He and his wife were carried off the train in St. Louis."

"Bad fish can kill a man," he remarked.

She gave a vigorous nod. "It killed poor Mr. Porter."

"What about Mrs. Porter?"

"She blamed everyone else for her husband's illness, even me. Can you imagine? I did warn him not to eat the fish, but he was most determined."

"Then why'd she blame you?"

"Because the Johnsons got sick. She didn't believe it was the food. She thought I was making everyone ill. You needn't fret about it, sir. If you don't eat any fish, I'm certain you'll be fine."

"Did the third couple eat fish too?"

She shook her head. "No, but it was still quite . . ."

"Tragic?" he supplied for her.

"Yes, tragic," she agreed. "How did you know? Have you heard what happened to Mr. Hanes then?"

"No, I was just guessing. What happened to Hanes?"

"He got shot."

"I knew you shot someone."

"I did not," she cried out. "Why would you think I'd do such a terrible thing?"

"You tried to shoot me," he reminded her.

"That was an accident."

He decided to humor her. "All right, then. Did you accidentally shoot Mr. Hanes?"

"No, I didn't. He and another man were playing cards, and suddenly one of them—I can't remember which one it was—accused the other of cheating. A fight ensued and Mr. Hanes was shot. He wasn't mortally wounded, and the other man could just as easily have been the one injured because they were both shooting their pistols at each other. It was very uncivilized. I ruined my best hat when I scooted under my seat with Mrs. Hanes so I wouldn't be struck by a stray bullet."

"Then what happened?"

"The conductor patched up Mr. Hanes's arm, stopped the train outside Emmerson Point and left him and his wife in the care of the town's doctor."

"And you came the rest of the way by yourself?"

"Yes," she said. "I'd go up to Golden Crest by myself too if I knew the way. The hotel proprietor told me I needed a guide, and so I've been looking for one. Then you offered your services. You are going to escort me, aren't you?"

"All right, I'll take you."

"Oh, thank you, Mr. Clayborne," she whispered. She clasped hold of his hand and smiled. "You won't be sorry."

"You may call me Travis."

"Very well. I appreciate your kindness, Travis, in escorting me."

"I'm not being kind. The way I see it, I'm stuck with you, and the sooner we get started, the sooner I'll be rid of you."

She pulled her hand away from his and turned to her luggage. "If I hadn't just remembered I'm not going to be honest and forthright anymore, I would tell you I think you're an extremely insolent and hostile man."

"You've been nothing but honest and forthright since you started talking, haven't you?"

"Yes, but I only just remembered not to be."

"I'm not going to ask you to explain this time," he

29

muttered. "Wait here while I get the horses. And by the way, Emily, you're only taking two satchels up the mountain. O'Toole will have to come and fetch the others. You can leave them in the hotel now. Olsen will make sure no one steals them."

"I'll do no such thing," she shouted so he could hear her. The rude man was already halfway down the street. "I'm taking every one of my bags, thank you very much."

"No, you're not, but you're welcome, anyway."

She gritted her teeth in frustration. She watched him stroll down the boardwalk, noticed how his shoulders and hips seemed to roll with each stride he took, and found his arrogant swagger most appealing. He was a striking fellow, all right. It was a pity he was also obnoxious.

With a sigh, she forced herself to look away. She was engaged to marry Mr. O'Toole, she reminded herself, and she shouldn't be noticing how fit any other man was.

She wasn't the alley cat in the family; Barbara was. Emily was the reliable and practical one, like an old but comfortable pair of shoes, she thought. No—she had always been reliable and practical in the past. She wasn't anymore.

Travis was just about to cross the street when she called out to him.

"Travis, I should warn you. I'm not at all reliable."

"I didn't think you were," he called out. "You don't have any sense either."

She smiled with satisfaction. That reaction stopped him dead in his tracks.

"You don't think I have any sense?"

Honest to God, she seemed thrilled by his assessment of her. Didn't the woman realize she was being given an insult?

No, not an insult, he qualified. Just the blunt truth.

"Emily?"

"Yes?"

"Does O'Toole know he's going to marry a crazy woman?"

Three

Emily was holding a grudge. Her glares and her stony silence were vastly amusing, but Travis didn't dare laugh or even crack a smile. She'd know then he thought her behavior was humorous, and he'd never hear the end of it.

She didn't speak to him again until they stopped in midafternoon to rest their horses. At least that was the excuse he'd given her. She seemed to believe the lie too. He really called a halt so that she could rest her backside. She wasn't much of a horsewoman, and the way her bottom kept slamming against her saddle, added to the pained look on her face, told him she was taking quite a beating.

The poor woman could barely stand up straight when she finally managed to get down to the ground.

She wouldn't let him help her and didn't think his exaggeratedly wounded expression was the least bit funny.

Because they'd ridden a good distance up the steep mountain path, the air was much colder. He took the time and trouble to start a campfire so she could shake off the chill. They ate a sparse lunch in silence, and just when he was beginning to think the trip wasn't going to be completely miserable, she went and ruined it.

"You did it on purpose, didn't you, Travis? Admit it, then apologize to me, and I just might forgive you."

"I didn't do it on purpose. You were supposed to hook your right leg over the pommel, remember? You were the one who insisted on riding sidesaddle. How was I to know you'd never done it before?"

"Ladies in the South ride sidesaddle," she announced.

He could feel a headache coming on. "But you're not from the South, are you? You're from Boston."

"What does that have to do with the price of pickles? Southern ladies are more refined. Everyone knows that, which is precisely why I've decided to be Southern."

He could feel the throbbing behind his temples. "You can't decide to be Southern."

"But of course I can. I can be anything I want to be."

"Why Southern?" he asked in spite of his better judgment.

"The little drawl in a lady's speech is considered very feminine and musical. I've done a complete study of it, and I assure you I know what I'm talking about. I believe I've perfected the drawl too. Would you like to hear me say—"

"No, I would not. Emily, not all southern ladies ride sidesaddle."

The glare she gave him made him sorry he'd brought up the subject of saddles again.

"Most southern women do," she said. "And just because I have never ridden sidesaddle before doesn't mean I couldn't have managed it if you hadn't interfered. You deliberately threw me over that horse, didn't you? I could have broken my neck."

He wasn't going to take the blame for her ineptness. "I merely gave you a hand up. How was I to know you'd keep on going? Is your shoulder still sore?"

"No, and I do appreciate the fact that you rubbed the sting out of it for me. Still, my dress is now covered with dirt, thank you very much. What will Clifford O'Toole think of me?"

"You've been wearing a pair of gloves with a large bullet hole through them. He'll probably notice that before anything else. Besides, if he loves you, your appearance won't matter to him."

She took a bite of her apple before she made up her mind to set him straight.

"He doesn't love me. How could he? We've never met."

He closed his eyes. Conversing with Emily was proving to be as difficult as trying to win an argument with his brother Cole. It was hopeless.

"You're going to marry a man you've never met? Isn't that kind of odd?"

"Not really. You've heard of mail-order brides, haven't you?"

"You're one of those?"

"Sort of," she hedged. She was, of course, but pride kept her from admitting it. "Mr. O'Toole and I have corresponded, and I believe I've come to know him quite well. He's an eloquent writer. He's a poet too."

"He wrote poems to you?" he asked with a grin.

Her chin came up a notch. "Why is that amusing?"

"He sounds like a . . . pansy."

"I assure you he isn't. His poems are beautiful. Will you quit grinning at me? They are beautiful, and it's apparent to me that he's a very intelligent man. You may read his letters if you don't believe me. I have all three of them tucked inside one of my satchels. Shall I fetch them for you?"

"I don't want to read his letters. You still haven't explained why you're so determined to marry a stranger."

"I tried marrying someone I knew, and look how that turned out."

"You decided on this course of action after you got jilted, didn't you?"

"Let's just say that it was the last disappointment I was going to suffer."

"Is that so?" he remarked, wondering how she was going to prevent further disappointments.

She seemed to read his thoughts. "I stayed up all that night . . . my wedding night," she said.

"Crying?" he asked.

"No, I didn't cry. I spent the entire night thinking about my circumstances, and I finally came up with a plan that I believe will change everything. I've always been forthright and honest. Well, no more, thank you very much."

"How come you're being honest with me?"

She shrugged. "I shouldn't be, I suppose. Still, I

won't ever see you again after today—at least I don't think I will—so it doesn't matter if you know I'm a fraud. No one else will."

"Trying to be something you aren't will only make things worse."

She didn't agree. "Being me didn't do me a lick of good, and once I figured that out, I decided to reinvent myself. I was sick and tired of working hard and being so boringly practical all the time."

"You're overreacting, that's all." *And crazy,* he silently added. "Your pride was wounded, but you'll get over it."

His cavalier attitude irritated her. "I know exactly what I'm doing, and pride doesn't have anything to do with my decision. Working hard hasn't gotten me anywhere. Shall I give you an example?"

She didn't wait for his answer, but plunged ahead. "Randolph was studying to become a banker. He was just beginning his last year at the university when we became officially engaged. His studies were difficult for him, and because of his grades, he was worried he'd be asked to leave. I told him that if he wouldn't accept every social invitation that came to him, he would have time for his studies, but he wouldn't listen to me. He asked me to help him with his research, and because I was such a ninny and wanted to please him, I ended up writing several lengthy papers for him. He was supposed to use the papers as his study guide, but I later found out he put his name on the top of the first page and handed them in to his professors. It was a dishonest thing to do, of course, and do you know what his punishment was? He took honors for his last year's work and was hired by one of the most prestigious banks in Boston. He started out making an impressive salary, and that was when my sister became interested in him. Ironic, isn't it? If I hadn't helped him, he wouldn't have gotten such a fine position, and my sister would have left him alone.

"I've learned from my mistakes though, which is why Mr. O'Toole and I are going to do well together. Randolph broke all the promises he made to me, and I won't let Mr. O'Toole ever break his word."

"How are you going to stop him?"

She ignored the question. "He might not be as rich as Randolph is, but almost, and he lives out here, in this beautiful, wild, untamed land, and that makes him just as appealing to me. I really hated living in the city. I could never seem to fit in. I know you don't understand because you've lived here all your life, but I felt as though I were suffocating. The air's dirty, the streets are crowded, and everywhere you look are buildings so tall you can't see the sky."

"Weren't you willing to live in Boston with Randolph?"

"He promised we would move west after one year of marriage. Father was horrified. He thought Randolph's handsome salary at the bank was far more important than my suffocation problems."

"Money isn't more important. I still remember what it was like living in New York."

Her eyes widened with surprise. "You lived in the East?"

"Until I was around ten or eleven years old."

"Why did you move?"

He was only going to answer her question and tell her a very little bit about his past, but she was such an easy woman to talk to, he got carried away and told her far more than he'd intended. He wasted a good half hour telling her about his brothers, his sister and her husband, and his Mama Rose. She seemed fascinated by his family and smiled after he mentioned he was going to become an attorney. He could have sworn tears came into her eyes when he told her Mama Rose was finally home.

"You're very fortunate to have such a loving family."

He nodded agreement. "What about you?"

"I have seven sisters. It's my hope that one day some of them will come and visit Mr. O'Toole and me. He has a grand house with a curved staircase. He told me so in one of his letters."

Travis didn't care about the house she was going to live in. "You'll be sorry if you marry a man you don't love."

She didn't show any reaction to his remark. He watched her thread her fingers through her hair. No matter how much she messed with it, the curls floated back around her face. She could be a real charmer all right. She was also an amazingly feminine creature, and if she could only learn to be a little less crazy, she'd be just about perfect.

He decided to tell her so. "You know what your problem is?"

"Yes, I do," she replied. "I should have learned from my sister. Barbara doesn't have a practical bone in her body. She doesn't have any common sense either. She pretends to be helpless too, and she's a marvelous flirt."

"No man wants a helpless woman, but a practical one is real handy to have around out here."

He stood up before she could start arguing with

him, stretched the muscles in his neck by rolling his shoulders, and then began to gather stones to put the fire out.

She surprised him by helping. It took only a couple of minutes to finish the task, and he was suddenly anxious to get going. He'd spent entirely too much time talking about himself and his family. He didn't understand why he'd told her so much, because it wasn't like him to ever tell an outsider personal facts.

He didn't consider Emily an outsider though. She was . . . different. He couldn't put his finger on what it was about her that got to him, but affect him she did, and in such a strange way his instincts warned him to keep his distance. His body had other ideas. He'd already had several fantasies about making love to her. He'd tried to picture her without her clothes on, which took quite a bit of imagination on his part, since she was covered from her chin to her toes.

He had a feeling she'd be spectacular. The way she filled out the top of her dress, the tiny waistband, and the narrow hips all suggested to him that she was well put together and that he wouldn't be disappointed. The woman had all the right curves and in all the right places.

Still, thinking about it and doing something about it were two different kettles of fish. He wasn't about to give in to his urges, but he didn't feel at all guilty picturing it in his mind. She was a sensual woman, and he appreciated a good-looking female as much as every other man living in the wilderness.

No, he wasn't concerned about his physical attraction to her. He could easily deal with that. What bothered him was the fact that he was actually beginning to enjoy her company, though why he liked being around a woman with such strange notions was beyond him. Emily made him smile, but only because she said the craziest things.

He enjoyed looking at her. Nothing wrong with that, he told himself. Why, it would have been wrong for him not to look. He was a healthy man with normal inclinations, and she was getting prettier by the minute. That didn't mean he was smitten with her.

He felt better once he'd analyzed his situation. He quit frowning too. He watched her feed the rest of her apple to her horse, thought it was a sweet, practical thing to do, and wondered if she had any idea how difficult it was going to be for her to keep up the pretense of being helpless around Clifford O'Toole.

He waited by the horses while she went to the stream to wash. He got a peculiar little catch in the back of his throat when she came running back to him. Her cheeks were rosy from washing in the cold mountain water, and she was smiling with pleasure over what she declared was a glorious day. He thought about kissing her then and there, and it took a good deal of discipline to keep his hands off her.

"I'm ready to go now, Travis."

He was suddenly all business. "It's about time. We've wasted almost two full hours here."

"It wasn't wasted time. It was . . . enjoyable."

He shrugged. "Do you want me to help you get up on your horse?"

"And get tossed over the top again? I think not."

She hopped about for a minute or two while she tried to anchor her foot in the stirrup, and just when he was going to demand that she let him assist her, she made it up into the saddle on her own. She gave him a victorious smile. It didn't last long.

"A helpless woman would have requested assistance," he said.

He was smiling as he swung up into his saddle. He must be crazy too, he decided, because he was beginning to really like Miss Emily Finnegan.

Four

❧

They didn't speak until they reached the gully he had hoped to use to shorten their journey, but just as Adam had predicted, it was flooded.

"You don't want to cross the river here, do you? Surely there's a bridge we could use."

"There aren't any bridges up here," he answered. "And this isn't a river, Emily. It's just a gully."

Her mount obviously didn't like being so close to the water's edge and began to prance about. Travis reached over, grabbed hold of the reins, and forced her horse closer to his side so he couldn't rear up.

"He must think he has to go in the water. He doesn't, does he?"

He could hear the worry in her voice. "No, he doesn't," he assured her. "We can't cross here."

His leg was rubbing against hers. She noticed, of course, but though she could have moved away, she didn't. She liked being close to him. He made her feel safe and yet uneasy too. What in heaven's name was the matter with her? She didn't seem to know her own thoughts anymore.

"We can't cross here." She repeated his words while she patted her horse in what Travis assumed was an attempt to reassure the animal.

"Now what?" she asked him.

"Your journey to Golden Crest has just been lengthened by at least two more days, maybe three."

It took all she had not to shout with relief. God help her, she was actually weak with it. It certainly was a peculiar reaction to hearing she wouldn't have to meet and marry Mr. O'Toole for at least two more days. She should have been disappointed over the news, shouldn't she?

Then why did she feel as though she'd just been given a stay of execution?

"Cold feet," she whispered.

"What did you say?" Travis asked.

She shook her head. "Nothing important," she said.

She wasn't about to tell him the truth. She wouldn't look at him either because she was certain he would be able to see the relief in her eyes. Travis already thought she was out of her mind to want to marry a complete stranger, and, honest to Pete, she was beginning to think he might be right.

Perhaps she was having before-the-wedding jitters. Some brides did, didn't they? Yes, of course they did, and all she needed to do now was read Mr. O'Toole's letters again. She was sure to feel better then. The man she was going to marry had poured his heart out to her and had proven beyond a doubt that he was a sensitive, caring man who would love and cherish her until death did they part. What more could she ever want from a husband?

Love, she admitted with a sinking heart. She wanted to love him as much as he claimed to already love her.

"You aren't getting sick on me, are you, Emily?"

"No, I never get sick. Why do you ask?"

"You're awfully pale."

"I'm just disappointed," she lied. "You must be disappointed too. It seems you're stuck with me for a couple of days. Will you mind?"

"No. Why are you so anxious to get to Golden Crest?"

"I should be, shouldn't I?"

"Did you love Randolph?"

The question jarred her. "What made you think of Randolph?"

He shrugged. "Did you?"

"I might have."

"What kind of answer is that? Did you like the way he kissed you?"

"For heaven's sake, it isn't appropriate for you to ask me such personal questions. It's going to rain soon, isn't it?"

"Yes, it is," he agreed. "Answer my question."

She let out a loud sigh to let him know she was becoming irritated with him before she finally acceded to his request.

"I didn't like or dislike them. His kisses were all right, I suppose."

He laughed.

"What did I say that you find so amusing?"

He didn't explain. Her answer had pleased him though. She hadn't liked being touched by good old Randolph if his kisses were just "all right."

"Where will we stay tonight?" she asked, trying to turn his attention so he wouldn't ask her any more personal questions.

"We'll have to backtrack a couple of miles and stay at Henry Billings's way station. The food's bad, but the beds are clean and dry, and if we hurry, we should get there before the rain starts. What are you staring at, Emily?"

"Your eyes," she blurted out, blushing because she'd been caught in the act. "They're very green. Did your brothers tease you when you were a little boy?"

"Tease me because of the color of my eyes?"

"No, because . . ." She realized what she was about to say and felt her face burn with mortification. Lord above, she'd almost asked if he'd been teased because he was so absolutely perfect. There'd be no living with him if she said that, she realized, and the rest of their journey would be filled with one vexing remark after another. She had already noticed he had a tendency toward arrogance.

"Tease me about what?" he asked again.

She stared up at him while she tried to come up with a suitable and impersonal remark.

"Being tall," she said.

He looked exasperated. "I wasn't tall when I was a child. I was short. Most children are."

"If you use that condescending tone in the courtroom, you're going to be a dismal failure. It's just a suggestion," she added when he frowned at her.

"Emily, if you keep looking at me like that, I'm going to get the notion you want me to kiss you."

"I don't."

"Then stop staring at my mouth."

"What would you like me to stare at, Travis?"

"The water," he snapped. "Stare at the water. You sure you don't want me to kiss you?"

The conversation was doing strange things to her. She couldn't seem to catch her breath. She knew she was daring the devil, but she couldn't make herself look away from him. She wasn't at all interested in staring at the water; she wanted to continue to stare at him. What was the matter with her?

"It probably wouldn't be proper for you to kiss me. I'm going to be married soon."

"You have no business marrying a stranger, Emily."

"Why do you care what I do?"

He didn't have a ready answer for the question. "I get bothered when someone does something I consider stupid."

"Are you calling me stupid?"

"If the hat fits . . ."

Five

Neither one of them said another word until they reached Billings's way station. Henry came outside the rectangular log cabin to meet them. He was a middle-aged man, as bald as a rock, and just about as talkative. He greeted Emily—at least she thought he did—but he mumbled so, she couldn't make out a word he said. He wouldn't look at her either. He motioned her to follow him inside and showed her where she would sleep by pointing toward a closed door.

The main room had bunk beds lined against every wall. A long wooden table with benches on either side was in the center near a potbellied stove.

Travis acted as though he and Henry were good

friends. During supper, he filled him in on all the latest news. Emily didn't say a word. She sat close to Travis's side at the table and tried to eat the foul-smelling soup she'd been offered. She couldn't get any of it down though, and since the proprietor wasn't paying any attention to her, she ate the brown bread and goat's milk instead and left the soup alone.

She excused herself as soon as she finished, but when she reached the door to her bedroom, she turned back to Travis.

"Will we reach Golden Crest tomorrow?"

He shook his head. "No, the day after," he said. "We'll stay with John and Millie Perkins tomorrow night. They rent out rooms in their home."

She told both men good night then and went to bed. Travis didn't see her again until she came outside the following morning with her satchel in her hands. She was wearing a pink dress with a matching sweater. The color suited her, and damn, but she was getting prettier and prettier.

He wanted to kiss her. He frowned instead and made a silent vow not to get near her today. He would keep the talk impersonal, no matter how much she provoked him.

The day's journey turned out to be extremely pleasant. Emily obviously didn't want to argue either, so the topics they ended up discussing were of a philosophical nature.

She confessed to being a voracious reader. He suggested she read *The Republic*. "It's all about justice," he explained. "I think you'll like it. I did. Mama Rose gave me a leather-bound copy along with a journal, and they're my most prized possessions."

"Why did she give you a journal?"

"She told me it was for me to fill with my accounts of all the cases I defend. She said that when I'm ready to retire, she wants me to be able to hold *The Republic* in one hand and the journal of my experiences in the other. It's her hope that the two will balance."

"Like the scales of justice," Emily whispered, impressed by the wisdom of Travis's mother.

She began to question him about Plato's work, and they debated justice and the law well into the afternoon. He thoroughly enjoyed sparring with her, so much so, he was sorry when the discussion ended.

It was his fault. He made the mistake of getting personal again.

"You're a contradiction, Emily. You've obviously been well educated, and I know you're smart . . ."

"But?" she asked.

"You're doing something that isn't smart at all. In fact, it's just plain stupid."

His bluntness got her all riled up. "I don't believe I asked for your opinion."

"You're getting it anyway," he replied. "You just gave me a passionate argument about honesty and justice, and surely you can see that the pretense you're thinking about pulling on your unsuspecting groom is downright dishonest."

It was the beginning of an argument that lasted until they reached the yard behind the Perkinses' house.

Travis did most of the talking. He gave her at least twenty reasons why she shouldn't marry O'Toole, but he believed his last reason was the most convincing one.

"You won't ever be able to keep up the charade of being a delicate little flower in need of pampering, Emily."

"I am delicate, damn it."

He snorted with disbelief. "You're about as fragile as a grizzly bear."

"If flinging insults is the only way you can argue your position, heaven help your clients."

Travis dismounted, then went to Emily's side and lifted her off her horse. His hands stayed around her waist much longer than necessary. "A good marriage takes effort, and honesty is a definite prerequisite."

"How would you know? You've never been married, have you?"

"That isn't relevant."

"Is flirting honest?"

He was caught off guard by her question and had to think about it for a minute before he answered. "Sometimes it's honest. Flirting is part of the courting ritual, but I personally think it's only honest when a woman flirts with the man she's set her cap on."

" 'Set her cap on'? Are you telling me you think she should only flirt with the man she's already decided to marry?"

"That's what I'm saying all right."

"That's ridiculous. Flirting is the first step in a long process of finding the right man or woman. Men flirt too, you know. They just don't do it the same way women do."

"No, we don't."

Arguing with him was proving exasperating. "It's all a game, isn't it, that's played out between men and women. It's harmless too. Besides, men like women who flirt with them," she added, remembering how

Barbara had always been able to get every available man at a party to flit around her as though she were their queen bee.

"No, we don't like women who flirt with us," he insisted. "We're much more intelligent than you think we are, and we sure as certain don't like being manipulated."

"You needn't use that superior tone with me. I've patiently listened to you argue your position for the past hour, and I never once scoffed at you. Granted, I wanted to, but I didn't. Now it's my turn. It's too bad I can't prove my point to you."

"What point?"

She knew he was deliberately trying to frustrate her and refused to cooperate. She stared at the buttons on his shirt so she couldn't be distracted by his smile, and said, "If the circumstances were favorable, I'd prove to you right this minute that a delicate little flower gets far more attention than a practical one."

"You really believe a helpless little woman who flutters her eyelashes and hangs on a man's every word will get his full attention?"

"I do."

"You're as nuts as a tree full of acorns."

She ignored his criticism. "I've done a complete study on this subject, Travis."

"What makes the circumstances favorable?" he asked, latching onto an earlier remark she'd made.

"Boston," she answered. She waved her hand toward the Perkinses' house as she continued. "I'm not about to draw any attention to myself in front of a crowd of strangers here because it would be foolhardy and perhaps even dangerous to do so. The men in Boston are more refined and know how to conduct themselves as gentlemen around ladies. There are rules, after all, and they abide by them. I can't say the same for the men who live out here because I don't know any of them."

"Most of the men out here are gentlemen, but there are a few who would think nothing of trying to drag you off with them. The way I see it though, being your escort means I'm responsible for your welfare, and I don't like the notion of getting into a fight just because you acted silly.

"Furthermore, we're about to eat, and I don't want to have to shoot anyone afterwards. It's bad for the digestion."

It was such an outrageous thing to say, she struggled to force herself not to laugh.

"Indigestion is the only reservation you have about shooting someone?"

"Just about," he told her.

"I don't believe you. You're teasing me, and a gentleman would never do such a thing."

"Now, Emily, we've been though this before. I know I mentioned I wasn't a gentleman. Fact is, you should be thankful I'm your escort."

She was so surprised by his matter-of-fact remark she didn't bother to push him away when he put his arms around her waist.

"Is that so? Why exactly should I be thankful?"

"Because if I weren't escorting you, I'd probably be one of the few who would drag you off with me."

She thought that was a lovely thing to say to her. He wasn't really serious. She shook her head at him to let him know she wasn't so gullible, then began to laugh. She stopped when she noticed he wasn't even smiling.

"We both know you aren't serious. Stop tormenting me. You wouldn't really . . ."

"You wouldn't have to flirt with me either."

"I wouldn't want to," she admitted. "Why are you holding on to me?"

"It makes it easier."

"Makes what easier?"

He slowly bent his head toward hers. "Kissing you."

He caught her whispered "Oh," as his mouth covered hers. His tongue swept inside to leisurely explore the sweet taste of her. She wrapped her arms around his neck and leaned into him. The last thought that fluttered through her mind was that she was going to insist that he let go of her just as soon as she finished kissing him back.

All that mattered now was Travis. She could feel his hard muscles under her fingertips and was a little overwhelmed by the sheer strength of him, yet he was being so incredibly gentle. She loved his masculine scent too. It did crazy things to her heart. She could feel it beating frantically now.

Lord, but he did know how to kiss.

He didn't understand why he suddenly felt the need to kiss her, but once the thought came into his mind, he couldn't get rid of it. He wasn't going to let passion get the upper hand, however, and as soon as the urge to become more aggressive entered his mind, he pulled away from her.

Damn, she was seductive.

Emily had a bemused expression on her face, but quickly came to her senses.

"You really can't kiss me whenever the mood strikes you."

To prove her wrong, he kissed her again. She let out a little sigh of pleasure when he lifted his head again.

"That was the last kiss you'll get from me," she announced, groaning inside over the shiver in her voice. "I mean it. You mustn't ever kiss me again." She added a frown to let him know she meant what she said.

"You were a willing participant," he said. "Or wasn't that your tongue inside my mouth?"

She turned scarlet within a heartbeat. "I was being polite."

He burst out laughing. "You are a piece of work, Miss Emily Finnegan. If I were the marrying kind, I'd give good old Randolph a run for his money."

She knew something was wrong with the comment he'd just made, but it took her a full minute to figure out what it was.

"Clifford O'Toole," she said then. "Randolph is the man who married my sister."

"Ah, that's right. The man who jilted you."

"Must you use that word?"

"No need to get in a huff about it," he told her.

Even though they were a good distance away from the barn, Travis could hear the squeak of the door as it was being opened from the inside, and he instinctively moved closer to Emily so he could shove her behind his back if he needed to. He didn't think he was being overly cautious, for he had learned from past experience that a few of the folks who visited the Perkinses' establishment lived like animals up in the high country and were a crude and uncivilized group who didn't abide by any man's laws.

Travis relaxed his guard as soon as he saw the man

strutting toward them. It was ornery Jack Hanrahan, whom everyone called One-Eyed Jack for obvious reasons. He was a fright to look at, with long straggly brown hair that hadn't been washed in years and a permanent scowl on his face that was mean enough to make a person think Jack was going to tear him apart. He was also downright vain about his godawful appearance and didn't bother to wear an eye patch. He thought a patch made him look sissified.

Every time Travis looked at Jack, he inwardly blanched. Other men weren't quite as restrained. They let Jack see their reaction, and that, according to old man Perkins, made Jack all the more vain. He got a kick out of terrorizing people.

Travis suddenly came up with one hell of a brilliant plan to make Emily come to her senses and realize how crazy her notions about men were.

"Maybe there is a way you can prove your point to me," he told her.

"There is?"

She tried to turn so she could see what Travis was staring at, but he put his hands on her shoulders and wouldn't let her move.

"Do you really want to show me how effective acting helpless can be around a man?"

"I would if I could. I've done a complete study on this topic, and I assure you I know what I'm talking about."

"Yeah, yeah. You studied it. How about proving it with the very next man you see?"

"You don't think I can do it, do you? Well, I can, Travis."

"You're that sure of yourself?"

"Yes, but only because I've watched it over and over again. My sister Barbara could turn all the men in a ballroom into a pack of fleas hopping around her, just like that," she said and snapped her fingers.

The comparison of Barbara to a dog made Travis laugh. "God help your husband if he ever does anything wrong. You sure do know how to hold a grudge."

"And just what does that mean?"

"Never mind." He gloated with satisfaction over what was going to be a well-deserved victory for all men everywhere. "Want to make it interesting and wager on the outcome?"

Although it wasn't proper for a well-bred lady to gamble, she was so certain she would win, she couldn't resist the temptation. Granted, she hadn't had much practice turning a man's head by acting helpless or coy, but she had observed the ladies traveling on the train who had blatantly flirted with several men, and she had also watched the master, Barbara, and therefore had complete confidence that she could pull it off.

"How much would you like to wager?"

"A dollar."

"Shall we make it more interesting and wager five dollars?"

"Five dollars, it is," he agreed.

"I want you to know I wouldn't agree to this if I thought the gentleman I'm going to give my attention to would end up with hurt feelings, but what I'm about to do is harmless. Wouldn't you agree?"

The thought of Jack Hanrahan getting his feelings hurt made Travis choke on his laughter. "Yes, it's harmless. Have we got a bet, then?"

"As long as it isn't dangerous," she hastily qualified.

"I won't let it be dangerous."

"What are the rules?"

"No rules," he replied. "Just a time limit. Is ten minutes enough time to turn a man into a blithering simpleton, or do you need more time?"

"Ten minutes will be just fine. Are you sure you don't want to set some other rules? I don't want you to accuse me of not playing fair."

"No other rules," he insisted. "Just flirt with the very next man you see," he told her before he slowly turned her around.

He heard her indrawn breath and was a little surprised she didn't scream. She took a step back toward him.

"You want me to flirt with . . . him?"

"His name's Jack Hanrahan, and he was the next man you saw, wasn't he?"

"Yes, but . . ."

Her shoulders were now pressed against his chest. He leaned down close to her ear and drawled out, "Did I happen to mention Jack's an avowed woman hater?"

She closed her eyes. "No, you did not. Is he dangerous?"

"He won't hurt you, or any other female, for that matter, but he sure won't be nice to you either. Folks say he has the personality of a rattlesnake, but I think that's a rotten thing to be saying about snakes. They're much sweeter. Do you want to admit defeat now, give me your five dollars, and be done with it?"

It was the combination of arrogance and laughter in his tone that swayed her. She straightened her shoulders and her resolve. Come hell or high water, she was going to get the man who looked like a barbarian to hang on her every word.

"He will be my finest challenge," she announced. "Stay here, Travis, and observe."

"Wait a minute. How will I know you've won?" he asked with another chuckle he couldn't contain, for the possibility of Jack being swayed by a woman was downright hilarious.

"Trust me. You'll know when I've won." She adjusted the folds of her skirt, straightened the collar on her blouse, and then took a deep, God-help-me breath.

Travis kept right on grinning as he watched her drag her feet toward her prey. He knew she had to be worried. Jack did look like a hungry bear who had just come out of his cave. He usually smelled like one too, and Travis couldn't help but think Emily was actually courageous to try to win him over. She was also being foolish and stubborn, of course, because she refused to admit that men were too intelligent to be taken in by a helpless woman.

"Be sure to do that thing with your eyes, Emily," he called out, pretending to be helpful.

She turned around. "What thing?"

"That twitching thing you did when we were in Pritchard. Jack will love that."

She wasn't amused. She whirled around and hurried toward the man she was determined to tame. By the time she reached him, her heart felt as though it was lodged in the back of her throat.

Whatever it was she was saying wasn't working. Jack kept right on scowling, God love him, and Travis could have sworn he heard him growl each time he shook his head at her.

Although ten full minutes hadn't passed, Travis decided to suggest to Emily that she give up. It really was hopeless, after all. He was just about to call out to her when One-Eyed Jack did the most vile, hideous thing. He smiled.

Six

❧

$\mathcal{T}$ravis blanched, blinked, and then looked again. The ugly smile was still there. He watched in disbelief as Jack thrust his arm out to Emily. She immediately hooked her arm through his and started walking by his side toward the house, smiling up at her escort.

Travis didn't think he could stomach much more. He did a double take when the mismatched pair reached him and he heard her chattering away in the most horrendous imitation of a southern drawl he'd ever heard.

"I declare, Jack, you're such a gentleman."

"I try to be, Miss Emily. I sure do like the way you sing your words."

"How sweet of you to say so," she replied with a

flutter of her eyelashes that made Travis lose his appetite.

"May I introduce you to my guide, Mr. Travis Clayborne, of Blue Belle?"

Jack quit grinning like a demented man long enough to flash his usual scowl at Travis. "I know you," he accused. "Didn't I shoot you a time or two, Clayborne?"

"No, Jack, you didn't."

"I recollect I did."

The set of his jaw indicated he was getting riled up. She quickly turned Jack's attention. "My, but I'm all tuckered out. Mr. Clayborne and I have been riding for hours and hours, and I'm not at all strong like you are, Jack. I'm too delicate for such strenuous activity."

Jack became solicitous once again. "Of course you're delicate. Anybody can see you ain't got much meat on your bones. Clayborne oughtn't to have set such a hard pace. Want me to shoot him for you, Miss Emily?"

The question so appalled her, she answered in a near shout. "No."

"You sure? I wouldn't mind none."

"I'm sure, Jack, but I thank you for offering. I'll be fine as soon as I sit down. I just need to rest for a spell."

"I'll get you settled in a comfortable chair in just a minute, Miss Emily. You sure do smell nice," he added in a rush.

"I declare, Jack, you'll spoil me with your compliments."

She didn't need to say another word or bat another eyelash. Travis listened as Jack promised to build her a fire so she could warm her feet, fetch her a drink so she could cool her parched throat, and bring her supper so she could regain her strength.

Travis wanted to shoot him. He felt justified too, because Jack had just disgraced every other man in the territory. Come to think of it, shooting was too good for him. Travis glowered as he followed the pair around the corner to the front stoop. The horses would have to be taken care of, but not until Travis knew who the other guests inside were and made certain Emily would be safe.

Jack opened the door for Emily and then, true to his nature, tried to kick it closed before Travis could come inside. It was a childish prank and one Jack so thoroughly enjoyed, he had to snicker about it.

John Perkins was standing in the hall waiting for them. He was a heavyset man with a triple chin, a potbelly, and a ready smile. He looked soft, but he was as tough as any other mountain man and didn't allow any nonsense inside his establishment. Any disputes that arose had to be settled outside, and from the number of unmarked graves on the hillside behind the house, it was apparent there had been a number of those fights in the past.

John usually greeted his guests. He couldn't seem to find his voice now, however, and appeared to be in a stupor as he stared in stunned disbelief at One-Eyed Jack.

John had apparently never seen Jack Hanrahan smile either.

"It's chilling, isn't it, John?" Travis remarked as he strolled past him on his way into the dining room.

John's wife, Millie, let out a little screech when she

spotted Jack grinning. Travis thought that was an appropriate reaction.

The dining room was deserted. Still, Travis insisted that Emily sit in the corner next to him with her back against the wall. One-Eyed Jack straddled the chair across from them, but he kept nervously glancing behind his shoulder to make certain no one was trying to sneak up on him.

John came to his senses before his wife did. He hurried to the table, his shotgun cradled in his arms, and stopped when he reached Travis.

"It's good to see you again," he remarked with another quick glance in Hanrahan's direction. "Millie, quit twisting your apron and come meet Travis's woman. Did you go and get yourself hitched?"

"No, Jack. I didn't get married."

He introduced Emily to the older couple and then suggested they both join them.

As soon as Millie had gotten over her reaction to seeing Jack smile, her attention moved to Emily. She seemed mesmerized by her, nervous too; Travis noticed the way she was fiddling with her hair and smoothing her apron.

When Millie was younger, she was quite attractive, and her good looks helped to soften her abrupt way with people. Age had made her features more angular and harsh, but the sparkle was still in her eyes.

"We might as well eat with our guests, Millie, seeing as Travis is a friend," John said. "If you can stop gawking at his woman long enough to fetch our supper."

Millie didn't budge. She gave her husband a look

Travis interpreted to mean John was going to catch hell later for teasing her.

"My hair used to curl the way hers does," Millie told her husband. "Might be it still would if it weren't so long."

"Expect you'll cut it, then?" John asked

Millie didn't answer her husband. She simply continued to give Emily her close scrutiny.

"Mr. Perkins, are you expecting trouble?" Emily asked, pretending not to notice that his wife was watching her every move.

"I always expect trouble," he replied. "That way I'm never taken by surprise."

"John started carrying a shotgun when he married Millie because he knew men would try to steal her away from him," Travis said.

"That was years ago," Millie interjected. "I was pretty then."

"You're prettier now," Travis told her. "John's still carrying his shotgun, isn't he?"

Millie blushed with pleasure and hurried out of the room.

"What are the two of you doing up in high country?" John asked with yet another worried glance at One-Eyed Jack.

"I'm escorting Emily to Golden Crest. She's meeting someone there."

Emily was relieved he hadn't given Mr. Perkins any other details.

Travis couldn't stomach looking at One-Eyed Jack's infernal grin another second.

"Emily, tell Jack to stop smiling. He's giving me the chills."

"I think his smile is charming," she replied. She

reached across the table and patted Jack's hand. "Don't pay any attention to him, Jack. He's just in a contrary mood."

"Want me to shoot him for you, Miss Emily?"

The question didn't faze her this time. "No, Jack, but thank you for offering."

Travis decided to ignore both Emily and Jack. He turned to John again and remarked, "You're light on guests tonight."

"We won't be light for long," John replied. "Ben Corrigan stopped by on his way home from River's Bend to visit with Millie and me for a spell, and he told me five men from Murphy's outfit are headed this way. They'll expect to spend the night, but if they give me any back talk at all, I'm tossing them out. They're all low-down, thieving troublemakers." He turned and raised his voice so his wife could hear him in the kitchen. "Millie, you'd better hide the money you've got tucked inside the cookie jar." Turning back to his guests, he said, "Travis, I'd keep an eye on your woman if I were you."

Travis nodded agreement. He didn't bother to correct John's misconception that Emily was his woman and, in fact, had to admit he kind of liked the sound of it.

The realization made him frown. She was soon going to be O'Toole's woman, he reminded himself, and he would probably never see her again.

"Looks like I won't be getting much sleep tonight," he said, accepting what he was going to have to do to keep Emily safe.

"Why is that?" Emily asked.

He doubted if she'd get any sleep either if he told her what Murphy's men were capable of, and so he decided not to answer her question and changed the subject instead.

"What other news did Corrigan have to tell you?"

"He mentioned there was a United States marshal poking around up here."

Jack Hanrahan's head snapped up, and he was suddenly mighty interested in the conversation. "What for?" he muttered. "The law ain't no good in these parts."

Jack was wrong, but neither John nor Travis felt inclined to tell him so.

"The marshal's searching for some men, and from the rumors Corrigan heard, they're about as bad as men can be. Word has it they've killed a woman and a child. The little girl was just three years old, and the bastards ought to hang for that. The marshal wants to haul them back to Texas to stand trial."

"The marshal's from Texas?"

"That's what Corrigan told me."

"Did he mention his name?"

"I don't recollect that he did. Why are you so interested in the marshal? I'd stay away from him if I were you. Corrigan said that when he was introducing himself to him, he was suddenly feeling real thankful he'd led such a law-abiding life. The marshal gave him the shivers, all right, with those cold blue eyes staring down at him. Corrigan told me he hopes he never runs into him again. That's what he said, all right."

"I'm looking for a man who goes by the name of Daniel Ryan. He stole something from my mother, and one way or another, I'm going to get it back. All Mama Rose remembers about him is that he's big, he has blue eyes, and he's from Texas."

"You aren't thinking the marshal's the man you're after, are you?"

John didn't give Travis time to answer him, but continued on. "It could be just a coincidence. Lots of men have blue eyes," he reasoned. "Maybe the gang he's after comes from Texas too, and one of them could have blue eyes."

"Mama Rose told me Ryan was very refined. They were close to our territory when they parted company at the train station, but he had already mentioned to her that he was headed north."

"I don't suppose the men the lawman's searching for are refined. Still, you could be climbing up the wrong tree, thinking the marshal's the thief. There might be other Texans roaming through these hills. You know how they like to bring their cattle up to graze on our land."

Travis shook his head. "None of them would bring their herds this high up the mountain. Besides, the man I'm looking for was spotted in River's Bend a couple of days ago, and didn't you say Corrigan had just come from there?"

"I did," John replied. "It sure looks like Corrigan met up with the man you're wanting, all right. If the Texan keeps to the northwestern trail, he'll have to come through this area, and you just might run into him too. If you don't mind my asking, what'd he steal from your mother?"

"A compass she was going to give to one of my brothers."

"A compass don't seem valuable," Jack said. "Is it?"

"It is to my brother," Travis told him.

"Maybe I'll steal it off the Texan and keep it for myself," Jack boasted. "Which brother was supposed to get the compass?"

"Cole."

"Never mind, then," Jack hastily decided. "I don't want him trailing me."

"You don't want any of the Claybornes trailing you," John said, clearly exasperated. "Not if you want to live to be an old man."

He turned back to Travis again and shook his head. "It isn't unheard of for a lawman to turn bad, but it sure makes me sick to think about it. It just isn't right."

"John, it's real doubtful the marshal is the man I'm looking for. I can't imagine a lawman putting his reputation on the line for such a petty crime. The compass is valuable, yet it's insignificant compared to the gold shipments and banknotes the marshal has surely recovered in the past."

Emily had listened to the discussion and couldn't resist offering her opinion. "If the marshal has your mother's compass, I'm sure he'll bring it back to her."

Travis couldn't resist teasing her. "That's what Mama Rose believes, and it's going to break her heart when she finally realizes she's been duped. The Texan has had plenty of time to bring it back. He's keeping it, all right. Still, I'm not certain the marshal is Daniel Ryan."

"I sure wish I'd gotten his name from Corrigan," John interjected.

Emily was becoming passionate about the matter. She shook her head at both men and said, "If the marshal accidentally took the compass, returning it is probably the last thing on his mind. Remember, he's searching for criminals."

"If he accidentally took it? What kind of an argument is that, Emily? No one accidentally steals anything."

"It could happen," she argued. "You're making assumptions based on nothing but a few paltry coincidences. Surely you can see that I'm right."

He hid his smile. Emily was filled with righteous indignation as she defended the man she had never even met. She was correct about jumping to conclusions, of course, but he wasn't going to tell her so. The debate would end then, and he was having such a good time arguing with her, he wanted to continue on. He liked the way her eyes sparkled whenever he said something she took exception to, and she found it impossible to make a point without waving her hands around, a trait he thought was delightful, even though he had to dodge getting hit a couple of times. He also liked the way her voice turned so earnest and trembled with her demand that he be reasonable.

Come to think of it, he liked just about everything about her. She was going to be difficult to leave in Golden Crest, and handing her over to another man was going to be almost impossible. The smile left his eyes as he pictured her in the arms of Clifford O'Toole.

With a good deal of effort, he was able to block the dark thought and turned back to John. "Did you ask me a question?"

John nodded. "I was wondering if the Texan told your mother he was a lawman."

"No, he didn't tell her what his occupation was."

"That's odd, isn't it?"

He saw Emily roll her eyes heavenward and decided to goad her by agreeing with John. "Yes, it sure is odd. I can't help but wonder why he'd hide it from her."

"You cannot know if he deliberately kept his occupation a secret or not," she cried out, her frustration apparent. "Neither one of you is being the least bit reasonable. I suggest that you stop believing the worst and have a little faith in the man."

"What for?" Travis asked. "He robbed my mother."

"It sure sounds like he did," John agreed.

"We take care of our mothers out here," Travis said.

"You're right about that," John said, and even Jack had to grunt his agreement.

"No one dupes our mothers and gets away with it," John said.

Emily gave up. There simply wasn't any way she could make them see how illogical they were being.

The men continued to discuss the situation for several more minutes, and then Travis asked John to keep Emily company while he saw to the horses.

"You don't need to worry about that chore. I hired a new hand, Clemmont Adam's boy, and I saw him through the window leading your horses into the barn. He'll take care of them and bring in your baggage too."

Emily wanted to wash before supper, and since Travis wasn't about to let her out of his sight, he went with her and made her wait while he washed up too. By the time the two of them returned to the dining room, Millie had already served the food and was sitting at the end of the table.

There was thick stew with biscuits and jam, coffee for those who wanted it, and cow's milk for those who didn't.

"I like to sit by myself when I eat," Jack told Emily. He lowered his head and stared hard at her when he added, "Then I got to get down to Cooper's place before dark."

She gave him a wide smile. "You've been very patient, Jack."

She turned to Travis and put her hand out to him with her palm up.

"I believe you owe me five dollars."

He was surprised she wanted to be paid her winnings in front of Hanrahan and Perkins. While he dug through his pocket for the money he owed her, he glared at Jack for disgracing him. From the curious look on John's face, Travis knew he was going to want to know why he owed her the money, and if Emily told him, Jack would know he'd been taken in by a woman.

There'd be real trouble then.

He put the money in her hand and was just about to tell John any questions he had would be answered later, when Emily turned his attention.

She handed the money to Jack. "Here you are, and thank you so much for your assistance."

"It wasn't too bad," Jack muttered. "Can I stop smiling now?"

"Yes, you may."

He looked relieved for a second or two before his scowl was back in place. Then he shoved his chair back, stood up, and carried his plate and his cup to the table at the opposite end of the room. Like Travis, the mountain man preferred to sit with his back against the wall so he could watch people coming and going without fear of being caught unaware.

Jack hunched over his plate and began to eat his stew with his fingers, but Travis noticed his full attention was centered on Emily. He seemed so taken with her he missed his mouth twice. The man had the manners of a pig, and Travis knew he wouldn't be able to eat his supper if he continued to watch him. He turned back to Emily.

"Let me get this straight. You told Jack what our bet was?" he asked, trying to sound outraged.

"Yes, I did tell him."

"Then I can only conclude you didn't think you could pull it off without his cooperation."

"I most certainly could have, but I didn't want to," she replied. "It wouldn't have been right to use Jack to win the bet. The men in Boston expect women to flirt with them, but Jack wouldn't have understood. No," she insisted, "it wouldn't have been right."

"Aren't you changing your tune?"

"No."

"Is that right? What makes Jack any different from Clifford O'Toole?"

"Let's leave him out of this, shall we?"

"Who is Clifford O'Toole?" John wanted to know.

"The man Emily's supposed to marry. Stop kicking me," he told her. "She hasn't met him yet."

"That doesn't seem right to me," Millie interjected. "Why would you marry a man you don't know when you're wanting another?"

"I don't want any other man," Emily said.

Millie snorted. "It's as clear to me as a clap of thunder that you're taken with Travis. Are you blind, girl?"

Emily could feel herself turning red with embarrassment. "You're mistaken, Millie. I barely know him. He's just my guide to Golden Crest."

Millie snorted again. Emily quickly tried to turn the topic back to the wager. She refused to look at Travis until she was certain he wasn't thinking about Millie's remarks.

"I won fair and square," she announced.

"You broke the rules."

She forced a laugh. "There weren't any rules, remember? You made that choice, not me."

"What was the wager?" John asked.

Travis paused to glare at Emily for kicking him again before he answered. He explained their argument and how he wanted to prove she was wrong.

"It was a foolish wager," Emily said. "But I did win, and it's all your own fault, Travis. You should have been more specific, like the moneylender in a story I read called *The Merchant of Venice*. Have you ever read it?"

"As a matter of fact, I have."

"I don't recall reading the story," John said. "Of course, I don't know how to read yet, and that could be why I don't recollect it."

"I don't recollect it either, John," Millie said. "But I'm wanting to hear about it."

"It's a wonderful story," Emily began. "A gentleman borrowed money and made an agreement to pay it back within a certain amount of time. He also agreed that if he wasn't able to repay, then he would give the moneylender a pound of his flesh."

John's eyes widened. "That would kill a skinny man, wouldn't it?"

"It would kill any man," Travis told him.

Out of the corner of his eye, he saw Jack get up and move to a table in the center of the room. It was apparent he was trying to get closer so he could hear every word Emily said, and he was also trying not to draw any attention to himself. It took all Travis had not to laugh, but, honest to God, seeing the savage up on his tiptoes really was comical. His brothers weren't going to believe him when he told them about it.

"Don't leave my John hanging for the rest of the story," Millie said in her usual abrupt tone. "It seems mighty foolish for a man to make such a rash promise, doesn't it, John?"

"Yes, Millie, it does seem foolish. Now, if the moneylender gave him time to put some weight on around his middle, well then, I'm thinking that promise wasn't so rash after all. Did he give him time?" he asked.

Emily shook her head and tried not to laugh. "No, John, he didn't give him time."

"He never should have made that promise," Millie insisted with a shake of her head. "He obviously wasn't from around these parts. Men out here would never do such a foolish thing."

"He was desperate," Emily explained. "And he was certain he would have the money in time to repay. He didn't though."

"I had a feeling that's what happened. Did he get cut up?" John asked.

"He died, didn't he?" Millie asked at the very same time.

"No, he didn't get cut up, and he didn't die," she answered.

"He welshed, didn't he? It just doesn't seem right to me," John said. "A promise made is a promise that's got to be kept. A man's word is sacred, after all. Isn't that right, Millie?"

"Yes, John, a man's word is all he's got in these parts. How did he get out of his promise?" she asked Emily. "Did he go into hiding?"

"No," Emily answered, smiling over the Perkinses' enthusiastic response to the story.

Travis was also smiling. Although he had read the Shakespearean play at Adam's insistence, he liked hearing Emily tell it much better. Her animated expressions made the characters seem real.

He happened to glance over at One-Eyed Jack then, saw what he interpreted to be a genuine smile on his face, and knew that Emily really had won the bet fair and square after all. The proof was hanging on her every word. Hanrahan was definitely smitten.

"If he didn't run away, what happened to him?" Millie asked.

"He refused to give a pound of flesh, and the moneylender refused to let him out of his promise or give him any more time, and so a trial was held to determine the outcome."

John slapped his hand down on the tabletop. "Leave it to the law to interfere."

"An attorney saved the man, of course," Travis said.

"Who just happened to be a woman," Emily reminded him. "Her name was Portia."

She and Millie shared a smile over that interesting fact before she continued.

"I'm wanting to know what in tarnation happened to the man who borrowed the money," Millie said. "What did the judge have to say?"

"He decided the agreement was legal and binding

and that the moneylender was entitled to his pound of flesh."

"I knew it, Millie. Didn't I tell you a promise made is a promise that's got to be kept?"

"Yes, you did, John."

"But," Emily hastily added before she was interrupted again, "it was also ruled that while the moneylender could take his pound of flesh, he couldn't take a single drop of blood."

John rubbed his jaw while he mulled the judgment over in his mind. "Well now, I don't believe you can take any flesh without taking some blood."

"It's a fact you can't," Emily explained. "If the moneylender had been more specific," she said with a meaningful glance at Travis, "the outcome might have been different, but he wasn't specific, and neither were you with our wager, Travis. I won fair and square."

He admitted defeat, told her there were no hard feelings, and even suggested that she gloat if she felt like it.

"Want me to kiss you to prove I'm not mad?"

He realized he'd embarrassed her as soon as she lowered her gaze to the tabletop and shook her head at him. He reached over and put his hand on top of hers.

"You've got a lot in common with Portia," he whispered. "But I don't think she blushed when she won her case. You have her passion though."

Emily was pleased by the compliment. She wasn't given time to thank him, however, for a loud thumping sound interrupted all of them.

Someone was trying to break through the front

door. John jumped up and ran to the entrance. Travis was right behind him.

"Are the men from Murphy's ranch here, Millie?" Emily asked.

"From the way they're banging on my door, I'd have to say it's them all right." She hurried over to Emily's side and latched onto her elbow. "You can finish eating in the kitchen tonight. You'll feel much safer, and Travis will make sure the ranch hands stay in my dining room. I don't know how I'm going to get you up those stairs though, but I'll let John worry about that. Come on, girl. This isn't the time to dally. Lord, I sure hope they aren't all liquored up. There's nothing worse than a drunk," she added with a shiver. "And if any of them steal my valuables, I swear I'll shoot them myself. Oh, I hope they aren't drunk."

Millie really was frightened. Emily wasn't about to take any chances. She picked up her plate of stew, followed Millie into the kitchen, and then offered to help her get the ranch hands' plates ready.

"You sit on down at the table and eat. I'll see to the chore after I put some more biscuit dough into my oven. After you've finished, you can scrub my frying pan if you have a mind to. It's been soaking in the basin long enough."

Emily was happy to have something to do. She quickly ate, then rolled up her sleeves and attacked the pan with a vengeance, smiling to herself as she tried to picture her mother's reaction if she were watching her daughter now. She would probably have heart palpitations, Emily supposed, for none of her daughters were ever allowed to do common housework—there were maids for that—but after she'd gotten over her initial shock, Emily didn't think she'd be disappointed in her.

"Millie, do you have anyone to help you with your chores?" she asked.

"No, but I'm getting used to the notion of hiring someone. My John's been nagging me to slow down, and lately our house has been packed with guests more often than not. After washing and cleaning and cooking and fetching all day long, by nightfall I'm so weary I can hardly get myself ready for bed."

"Have you ever thought about moving to a town?"

"No, I'd never want to do that. Folks have to come through here to get north or west unless the season's dry and they can cut through the gullies, and even though we have lots of company, we're still isolated enough to feel free. I don't think I could abide having neighbors living right on top of me, knowing my business. John wouldn't like it either."

Emily had lifted the heavy pan out of the soapy water and begun to dry it with the towel Millie handed her when she suddenly noticed the pounding had stopped. She also noticed Millie's hands were shaking.

"Do you think Murphy's men have left?"

"We aren't going to be that lucky. Their kind never gives up."

"Exactly what is 'their kind'?"

"Ignorant drunks who steal anything that will bring a dollar for more liquor and break everything else. Can't reason with a drunk, Emily, but don't fret about it. Your man won't let any harm come to you."

"He won't let anyone hurt you either. He isn't my man though," she said.

"You're wanting him to be, aren't you?"

Her bluntness made Emily smile. "Why would you think that? I'm on my way to marry another man," she reminded her.

"Don't seem right to me," Millie muttered. She shut the oven door and turned so Emily could see her frown. "You seem smart enough, girl. You'd best rid yourself of your pride and tell him what's inside your heart before it's too late."

"But, Millie . . ."

"Won't do you any good to argue with me. There were sparks flying between you two, and anyone with half a brain would know what's going on. Ask him to court you."

Emily shook her head. "Even if I did want Travis to court me, it wouldn't matter. He told me he isn't the marrying kind."

Millie scoffed at the notion. "No man's the marrying kind until the ceremony's over. Don't you go believing that nonsense, girl. I saw how close he sat next to you at the table. Why, he had you squeezed up nice and tight against his side. I saw him take hold of your hand too, but I didn't see you pull away. You didn't mind one little bit, did you?"

Emily's shoulders sagged when she said, "No, I didn't mind. I don't know what's come over me. Mr. O'Toole's letters were very nice, and when he suggested—"

"Hogwash," Millie muttered. "Are you going to ruin your life because of some letters?"

"It wasn't supposed to get complicated," Emily said. "I made up my mind to take charge of my destiny, and now I think that maybe Travis was right.

He told me it was my pride being wounded that made me act so rashly. Millie, I don't know what to do. I like Travis, but I'm certainly not in love with him. Why, I've only known the man for a couple of days, and we've spent most of our time together arguing about this and that."

"Love can happen quick," Millie told her. "I took one look at my man, and I knew I was going to nab him."

Emily didn't want to "nab" anyone. The conversation was making her agitated, for Millie was forcing her to think about things she would rather ignore. Emily wanted to convince herself that she was simply getting cold feet again, but she quickly recognized the lie. Dear God, what was happening to her? She didn't know her own mind anymore.

"You're very fortunate to have found John," she said. "How did you meet him?" She added the question in hopes of turning Millie's attention away from her conflicting feelings about Travis.

Millie was just about to answer her question when the back door flew open and slammed against the kitchen counter, causing both women to jump in reaction. Two of the scruffiest looking creatures Emily had ever seen came sauntering inside. Millie let out a very unladylike blasphemy that so surprised Emily she turned to look at her.

The creatures quickly recaptured her full attention, however.

"No one's keeping us out," one of the men said. He let out a loud belch before he added, "Ain't that right, Carter?"

The other creature was too busy staring at Emily to

answer his friend. "Look at what we got here, standing in front of the cabinet John hides his liquor in, Smiley."

Emily was trying hard to blend into the wall. The men reeked of foul whiskey and were swaying on their feet as they gawked at her, and she knew it would only be a matter of minutes before they both passed out. She decided to humor them until then, or until Travis and John came into the kitchen and tossed them out.

She tucked the frying pan behind her while she stared back at them. She couldn't make up her mind which one was uglier. Smiley's teeth were so rotten they'd turned black in spots, which made his smile all the more repulsive. He drooled too.

Carter wasn't any prize either. His head appeared to be too big for his squat body, and there was a stench about him that was so horrid, Emily actually gagged.

Compared to these two, One-Eyed Jack was a ladies' man.

Millie's profanity hadn't made much of an impression on them. Neither one even bothered to glance her way.

"I'm wanting at that whiskey," Smiley muttered.

"Me too," Carter agreed. He licked his thick lips in anticipation, then made a smacking noise that Smiley found so comical he started chuckling, and if the raucous noise the two of them were making wasn't bad enough, watching the spittle from Smiley's mouth dribble down his chin was simply more than Emily could stomach.

Lord, they were vile.

Emily was simmering with anger. She wasn't going to let her temper get the upper hand though. Caution was prudent now, she decided. It would be foolhardy to provoke them, for even though she had never seen a drunken man up close, she had heard that they were all unpredictable, and Millie had just told her it wasn't possible to reason with a drunk.

She really wished she had a weapon close-by, then realized she was gripping one in her hand. The frying pan could do enough damage to send them running, and she wouldn't have the slightest qualm about using it if either one of them tried to steal so much as a speck of dust.

"Please leave. You're frightening Millie."

"We ain't going nowhere until we're good and ready," Carter muttered.

Smiley snorted agreement.

"I'm wanting at that liquor," he whispered to Carter loud enough for both women to hear. "If I got to toss the woman out of my way, I will. No one comes between me and my whiskey."

Carter vigorously nodded agreement. The movement must have made him dizzy, because he started swaying in a circle.

"I'm wanting the money tucked inside the cookie jar," he told his cohort. His gaze searched the room before he added, "Millie went and hid it on us."

"Guess we got to tear the place apart to find it then."

Carter snickered. Millie straightened her shoulders but continued to give away her fear by twisting her apron. "You get on out of here, both of you, or I'll shout for John."

Carter pulled his bowie knife from his waist-band and waved it at her. The stupid man was so drunk Emily was amazed he could hold on to the weapon.

"You keep your trap shut, or this here knife is going in your belly," he hissed.

Millie's complexion turned as white as the dishcloth. Seeing her fear fueled Emily's anger. How dare they come into this dear woman's home and threaten her?

Emily took a deep breath. Oh, what she would have given to have John's shotgun now. She'd shoot both of them for upsetting poor Millie. She wouldn't kill them though; she'd just make it painful for them to walk for a long time.

"Let's get the pretty little heifer out of our way," Smiley suggested to his friend.

Emily blinked. In the space of Millie's loud indrawn breath, she went from anger to fury.

"What did you just call me?" she asked, her voice a strained whisper.

Her eyelid began to twitch while she waited for him to repeat the insult.

"A pretty little heifer," Smiley told her.

She drew herself up to her full height and glared at the men. Caution be damned.

"Millie? I can't seem to make up my mind. Which one do you think is uglier? The one with the black teeth or the one with the fat head?"

Millie let out another gasp. Her eyes looked as though they were about to pop out of her face. "Are you trying to get them mad, girl?"

Smiley took a step toward Emily. "She's Travis

Clayborne's woman," Millie cried out. "If you touch her, he'll kill you."

"We ain't got no quarrel with Clayborne," Smiley muttered. "He won't know what happened until it's too late. He's busy with the others out front, and we'll be long gone with our whiskey and money before he comes inside. Ain't that right, Carter?"

"We can ride fast when we got to," his friend boasted. "Go and push the little heifer clear into the dining room. I'll back you up."

Millie started to slowly edge her way to the table, hoping she could duck underneath to protect herself from Carter's knife while she screamed for her husband. Out of the corner of her eye she noticed Emily wasn't trying to back away from the man stalking her.

"Run," Millie cried out.

Emily shook her head. "Not until I help you take the garbage out."

The remark made Smiley stop. He swayed on his feet, staggered backward, then turned to Carter. "Is she talking about us?"

"What's come over you?" Millie whispered.

"Anger. I don't appreciate being called a cow; I don't like being threatened, and I hate the way they're scaring you," Emily answered. She kept her gaze on the drunks. "Millie has asked you to leave. Please do as she says."

Smiley snorted. He put his arms out at his sides and tried to rush her. He was so drunk, he bounced against the counter twice and lost more distance than he'd gained.

"Get behind my back," Millie shouted.

Emily was too busy at the moment to explain she wasn't about to do such a cowardly thing. Timing, after all, was everything. She nervously waited until Smiley was just about two feet away from her, then swung her arm in a wide arc and slammed the frying pan up against the side of his head.

Spittle went flying every which way as Smiley staggered backward, screeching like a wounded rooster, before he finally collapsed in a heap on the floor.

Carter was so taken aback by her attack he dropped his knife. "You knocked him stupid," he bellowed.

"No," Emily corrected in what she believed was a reasonable tone of voice. "He was already stupid. I knocked him out."

Her heart was frantically pounding, and her hand shook as she lifted the hem of her skirt, stepped over the prone man, and continued on toward his cohort. She had to get to him before he remembered he'd dropped the knife, or both Millie and she were going to be in real trouble.

Carter wasn't as drunk as she thought he was. Quick as a pistol shot, he squatted down, scooped up his knife, and snarled at her like a mad dog.

Emily took a hasty step back. Millie tried to help her by throwing everything she could get her hands on at Carter. He ducked the cup and saucer she hurled at him, but the copper kettle clipped him on his shoulder.

He let out a howl of pain, his gaze shifting back and forth between his two adversaries. Emily thought he was trying to decide which one to go after first. Millie drew his attention when she started screaming her husband's name over and over again. Emily seized the opportunity and slammed the frying pan into his elbow. She let out a yelp of dismay, for she'd tried to knock the knife out of his hand and had missed by an arm's length.

Carter shouted with rage, and from the look in his eyes, she knew his intentions had just turned deadly.

Seven

He never touched her. One second she was staring at his ugly expression and the next she was looking at Travis's broad back. He seemed to have appeared out of thin air, and though she didn't have the faintest idea how he'd managed to get in front of her without making a sound, she was so happy to see him she patted his back.

The odds, after all, had just improved considerably. Emily moved to his side just in time to see his fist strike Carter below his chin. The force behind the blow was so powerful it sent him flying out the doorway through the screen. He landed on his back in the grass with his legs draped over Millie's butter churn.

Travis wanted to hit him again. He was so furious

he was shaking. When Jack told him there were two men in the kitchen threatening Emily, Travis became enraged. He got scared too, and that enraged him all the more. His heart felt as if it was going to jump out of his chest as he raced toward the house. When he saw the son-of-a-bitch waving a knife in Emily's face, something snapped inside of him, and he suddenly wanted to tear her attacker apart limb by limb.

The idea still appealed to him. For a full minute he kept his attention on the man he'd knocked senseless, willing him to get up so he could hit him again, but the drunk didn't cooperate. He was out cold, and Travis finally accepted the fact that he wasn't going to be able to beat the hell out of him.

He turned around, put his hands on Emily's shoulders, and asked her to look up at him.

"Are you all right?" His voice was a rough whisper. "He didn't hurt you, did he?"

"No, he didn't hurt me," she answered, surprised at how weak her voice sounded.

He noticed the iron pan in her hand then, took it away from her, and put it on the counter.

Emily suddenly needed to sit down. Now that the danger had passed, the reaction hit with a vengeance. Her knees went weak and she was suddenly shivering with cold. She turned away from Travis, pulled out one of the kitchen chairs, and plunked herself down on the seat.

John came running into the kitchen. He looked at his wife first, saw that she was all right, and turned to survey the damage. His gaze shifted back and forth between the remnants of the screen door and the man sleeping spread-eagle on his floor.

Emily watched him shake his head as he pulled his wife into his arms and hugged her. Emily wished Travis would put his arms around her, hold her tight, and comfort her in much the same way John was comforting his wife. Did the Perkinses know how fortunate they were to have found each other?

John placed a kiss on Millie's forehead before once again turning to the unconscious man littering his floor.

"What happened to him?"

Millie joined Emily at the table before she answered him. She sat down with a loud, weary sigh, and then said, "She's what happened to him." She pointed at Emily to emphasize the fact. "John, I don't know what came over her. One minute she was trying to squeeze herself into the wall, and the next minute she was banging my best frying pan up against his head. It was something he said that set her off."

Travis leaned against the counter, folded his arms across his chest, and stared down at Emily. He watched her lower her gaze to her lap and noticed a faint blush cover her cheeks.

He couldn't understand her timidity now. "Emily, are you embarrassed about something?"

She answered with a dainty shrug of her shoulders. He didn't have the faintest idea what that gesture was supposed to mean. She'd acted like a wild mountain cat moments before, ready and willing to do as much damage as she could with her frying pan, and though Travis had kept his attention on the drunk threatening her with a knife, he had noticed the determined glint in Emily's eyes when he'd moved to stand in front of her.

Now she was acting like a woman who could swoon at the drop of a hat.

John put his hand on Millie's shoulder and gave her an affectionate squeeze. "I'm going to put a strong bolt on that door before I go to bed. I don't know what I'd do if anything happened to you."

"I'm not embarrassed. I'm ashamed. I deliberately provoked them."

Travis was the only one who heard Emily's whisper. "How did you provoke them?"

"I lost my temper. I shouldn't have though, because I put Millie in danger."

"How'd you do that?" John asked.

"She did no such thing, John," Millie said.

"Yes, I did. I incited them," Emily argued. "I deliberately made them angry by telling them how ugly I thought they were."

Travis squatted down beside her and took hold of her hands. "Look at me," he ordered.

She lifted her gaze to his. "I should have tried to placate them, but they made me so angry. One of them called me a heifer."

A hint of a smile crossed his face. "A heifer?"

"That's what did it, all right," Millie interjected. "She got that mean look in her eyes right after that one named Carter called her a 'pretty little heifer.'"

Emily straightened her shoulders. "No woman likes to be called a cow," she announced in her haughtiest voice.

Travis and John both tried to hide their grins. Millie shook her head. "I think he was complimenting you in his own vile way. He didn't call you a cow,

Emily. He called you a pretty heifer," she reminded her.

"Correct me if I'm wrong, but aren't they the same thing? Travis, I don't believe I've said anything amusing. Why are you smiling?"

"Your indignation," he replied.

John insisted on hearing every detail, and Millie was happy to oblige. Travis listened as he dragged Smiley out of the kitchen and shoved him into the grass next to his friend. His attention kept returning to Emily, and after he'd finished his chore, he leaned against the doorframe and blatantly stared at her.

She had been shivering a few minutes before, but under his close scrutiny, she was feeling uncomfortably warm in no time at all. She was also having difficulty drawing a deep breath.

John drew her attention when he pulled out a chair and sat down next to his wife. Emily watched him put his hand on top of Millie's, and it was that simple, little gesture of affection that proved to be her own undoing. She was suddenly so consumed with such hot, painful longings for Travis, she wanted to weep. She couldn't understand what was happening to her. She had never had lustful, carnal thoughts before, but she was certainly having them now, and how was that possible? Why was she yearning for something she had never experienced?

Emily made the mistake of looking at the man who was responsible for her misery. The sight of him only intensified her erotic thoughts, and she hurried to look away.

She wasn't quick enough though. Wanting him was

bad enough. What made it worse was that she was certain he knew it. The dark look in his eyes told her so.

She jumped to her feet, nearly overturning her chair in her haste. She needed to get busy, she told herself, to take her mind off her outrageous daydreams. She decided to clean up the mess around her, but Millie paused in her story to insist that Emily sit back down.

She was simply too agitated to sit anywhere, and so she stood by the entrance to the dining room instead. She was deliberately trying to put as much distance between herself and Travis as possible. She didn't dare look at him again, so she pretended grave interest in Millie's every word.

And, Lord, it was hot in the kitchen.

"John, what took you and Travis so long to get in here?" Millie asked.

"We had our hands full; that's what took us so long," he replied. "Corrigan told me five men were heading this way, but he was wrong about the number. There were eight of them out front trying to get inside, and all but two were stinking drunk. We didn't know a couple of others were sneaking up on the back door. I sure did itch to shoot them, Millie."

"What held you back?" she asked.

"Four of them decided to take Travis on, and all at the same time. They came at him from every direction, putting him right in the thick of it."

Emily's eyes widened, and she couldn't stop herself from looking at Travis. "You were in the thick of it? You don't have a mark on you."

"His fists have got to be tender," John interjected.

"I had to keep my shotgun trained on the other hooligans so they wouldn't try any nonsense on me. It was a real fracas, I'm telling you, and One-Eyed Jack was the only one enjoying himself. He looked like he was having a mighty fine time. As pretty as you please, he sat himself down on my front stoop, until he remembered seeing two of the men going around back. We would have gotten here sooner if Jack hadn't been so preoccupied."

Emily enjoyed the way John painted a story. She could picture Jack slapping his knee in amusement while he watched the fight, and she almost burst into laughter then. The contrary mountain man was unlike any other man she'd ever met.

"I'm glad he finally remembered," she said.

"Didn't you hear me shout for you, John?"

"Now, Millie, with all the commotion going on out front, how could I hear you?"

"If you hadn't come inside when you did, I don't know what would have happened," Emily admitted.

"You were holding your own," he told her.

"Millie, I'm so sorry I scared you."

"You didn't scare me. You sure did surprise me though. I forgot all about the frying pan until you whacked it upside his head."

"We'd better put her in the corner room, don't you suppose, Travis?" John asked. "No one can get to her through the window, and I imagine you'll hear anyone coming down the hall. I don't suppose those two sleeping it off in my backyard will sober up enough to come after Emily, but we shouldn't be taking any chances."

"Are you going to let Murphy's men sleep inside tonight?" Emily asked.

"Just the two who aren't drunk," John explained. "I'll put them at the opposite end of the house, so you don't need to worry. Travis will be in the room next to you."

John's last remark wasn't at all comforting. Having Travis so close seemed as dangerous to her as having Smiley in the next room. Travis wouldn't hurt her, of course, and he wouldn't force himself on her either, but then he wouldn't have to, would he? The mere thought of being alone with him did crazy things to her heart, and she could hear the warning bells ringing loud and clear in the back of her head.

Travis moved away from the door. "I'll show her where her room is," he remarked, completely ignoring Emily shaking her head at him.

He caught hold of her hand and continued on into the dining room. She tried to pull away from his grasp, but he tightened his hold to let her know he wasn't letting go.

Jack hovered near the front door, waiting for Emily. "I'm wanting to leave now," he announced.

Emily smiled at him. "Thank you again for going along with my game, Jack."

"I'm wanting to shake your hand before I leave," he muttered. "Unlatch her for a minute, Clayborne. I'm not going to steal her."

Travis let him have his way. He watched the two of them shake hands and couldn't help but notice the surprised look on Emily's face.

Jack leaned close to her, whispered something into her ear, and then pulled away. "I might be running into you again real soon," he predicted. He shoved his hat on his head, turned around, and stomped out the front door.

Emily hurried to get around Travis before he tried to grab hold of her again. She bent down to pick up the hem of her skirt and then went upstairs.

Travis stayed right behind her. "What did he say to you?"

She reached the landing, turned around, and held out her hand.

Travis saw the five dollars and started laughing. "I knew Jack was taken with you, but I never thought he'd give you your money back."

"He's a dear man."

He looked exasperated. "No, he isn't. He's a cantankerous old goat. He smells like one too. He sure does like you though."

"I like him too," she assured him.

Because he stood on the step below her, they were almost eye-to-eye. All she could think of was moving into his arms and kissing him. Emily realized then that she was staring at his mouth. Dear God, he was bound to know what she was thinking. It was all his fault, she decided. If he weren't such a handsome rogue, she surely wouldn't be having such impossible thoughts now.

"I'm tired tonight," she blurted out.

"You should be tired. You had your hands full with those drunks in the kitchen."

"I was scared."

"There isn't anything wrong with being scared. You used your wits."

Where in thunder were her wits now, she frantically wondered. Travis was turning her into a nervous twit, and if she didn't get away from him soon, heaven only knew what she would do.

She quickly turned around. "You don't need to follow me to my room. I'll find it by myself."

If he noticed her voice trembled, he didn't say anything about it. He caught hold of her hand and led her down the dark hallway to the door at the end of the corridor.

His arm brushed against hers as he leaned past her to open the door. "Your bags are probably inside."

"Yes, they probably are," she replied for lack of anything better to say.

Travis glanced inside and then nodded. "They're in the corner by the window."

"Your satchels," he explained when she gave him a puzzled look.

She shook herself out of her stupor and hurried inside. Travis stayed in the doorway. He knew he should pull the door closed now and walk away. He couldn't make himself move though, and, God help him, he couldn't stop staring at her either.

She was standing entirely too close to the bed, and he was rapidly coming up with all sorts of possibilities.

His voice dropped to a whisper. "If you need anything, let me know."

"Thank you."

"Good night, Emily."

"Good night, Travis," she whispered back.

And still he didn't move. She took a step closer to him. "It's hot in here, isn't it?"

"Are you hot?"

"Yes."

"Me too."

"Where are you sleeping?"

"Close-by," he answered. "I'll hear you if you call out."

"I won't."

"But if you do . . ."

"You'll hear me."

"Yes."

"I'll try not to bother you."

His smile was devastatingly appealing. "I'm already bothered, Emily, and from the way you're looking at me, I'd say you're real bothered too."

She didn't try to pretend she didn't know what he was talking about. She took another step toward him just as he moved toward her. And suddenly she was in his arms and she was kissing him with all the passion she had inside her.

One kiss wasn't enough. Frantic to get as close to him as possible, she wrapped her arms around his neck. Her fingers gripped his hair while his mouth ravaged hers.

He couldn't get enough of her. He lifted her up so she was pressed tight against him, but the feeling he wanted was dulled by their clothing.

He groaned in frustration and began to take her clothes off, but his mouth never left hers. She was so hot and willing, and God, but she tasted wonderful to him. He unbuttoned her blouse, tore it free of her waistband, and then pushed the straps of her undergarment down over her shoulders. His hand moved beneath the fabric and began to stroke her breast.

The feel of her smooth skin against the calluses on

his hands pushed his control further away. She made him so hot for her, he could barely think now. He wanted her more than he'd ever wanted any other woman before.

Travis kicked the door shut with his foot, forced himself to pull back from her, and then told her in no uncertain terms what he wanted to do to her.

He had to hold her up when he was finished. "Yes or no, Emily?" he demanded.

She didn't want to make the decision. He was forcing her to be accountable for her own actions, and she would much rather have been swept off her feet instead.

Admitting the truth helped her come to her senses. She pushed away from him and shook her head. "No, we can't. I want to, Travis, but it wouldn't be right."

She was panting now and still couldn't seem to draw a deep breath. She threaded her fingers through her hair in acute frustration.

His own frustration made him sound angry. "Because of O'Toole?"

"Who?"

He clinched his jaw tight. "The man you're going to marry."

She noticed her blouse was open and frantically rebuttoned it. "I used to have morals until I met you, Travis. I don't know what's happened to me."

"Lust happened. That's all there is to it, Emily."

"Don't be angry with me."

"I'm not angry with you. I never should have let it go this far." He pulled the door open, then turned back to her. "You wanted me, didn't you?"

"You know I did."

He saw the tears in her eyes and was heartless to them. "You know what I think? When you're in bed with O'Toole, you're going to be thinking about me."

The door slammed shut on his prophecy.

Eight

She hated him because he was right. She was never going to be able to forget him, and if she married Clifford O'Toole, every time he touched her, she would be thinking about Travis.

Their marriage would be a mockery, of course. Mr. O'Toole was bound to be miserable and so was she, though probably no more miserable than she was now.

She tossed and turned in the double bed for several hours while she thought about the mess she'd made of things. She wanted to blame Travis for complicating her plans, but she was honest enough to admit it was her own wounded pride that had landed her smack in the middle of this mire. When Randolph left her wilting at the altar, Emily had been so mortified and embarrassed she'd run headlong into another engagement. She wasn't devastated by Randolph's betrayal. She had never loved him, and it was her own stupid pride and stubbornness that had kept her from admitting it.

What a fool she'd been. She remembered boasting to her parents that she was the one who was responsible for her own future and no one else. She had truly believed that she could control her own destiny and had diligently tried to do just that, with disastrous results. In less than one short week, everything had gotten all twisted around on her, thanks to Travis.

Her destiny had definitely run amuck, and all because she was falling in love with the wrong man. How could such a thing happen so quickly? Love was supposed to build slowly over time, wasn't it? No one ever really fell in love at first sight. Why did she have to be different? Well, her attraction to Travis didn't matter. She wasn't about to let it go any further and tried to convince herself that it was merely an infatuation on her part and nothing more. He'd called it lust, she remembered, and she thought she'd like to bang Millie's frying pan up against his thick head right this minute for believing such a thing. Perhaps then he would have an inkling of the pain he was causing her.

She was appalled by her own shameful thoughts. She had never had violent notions in the past, but then she hadn't known Travis either, and the two did seem to go hand in hand. It was all his fault that she was so miserable, for not only was he trying to steal her heart, he was also turning her into a shrew with criminal inclinations. Why, by the time Travis had left the bedroom tonight, she'd entertained the notion of shooting him in the backside, where, she was certain, his brain was located.

Emily threw off her covers, got out of her bed, and began to pace around the room. What in heaven's name was she going to do about Mr. O'Toole? She couldn't marry him, of course, but how was she going to tell him? She considered writing a letter to him to explain her change of heart, then decided that a cold, impersonal note was a cowardly way out. She certainly hadn't appreciated getting a note from Randolph and Barbara, and she sincerely doubted Mr. O'Toole would appreciate one either. Like it or not, she was going to have to face him when she told him, and all she could do now was fret about it and pray that she could come up with the right words to use so he wouldn't feel she had betrayed him.

Whispers coming from the hallway turned her attention. She tiptoed over to the door, leaned against it, and then heard what sounded like a gun being cocked. There were at least two men in the corridor, perhaps as many as three. One of them was Travis, for she recognized his whisper. Whomever he'd spoken to left in quite a hurry and didn't try to be quiet about it. His boots pounded on the wooden floor as he retreated.

She heard a door slam then. She didn't hear Travis leave though. She battled her curiosity for a long minute and then decided to find out what he was doing.

She was slowly turning the doorknob when he spoke to her.

"Go back to bed, Emily."

She let out a yelp and jumped a good foot. She pulled the door open wider, forgetting for the moment that she was clad in only her nightgown, and when she saw Travis, she took a step back.

He was right outside her door, sprawled on a chair. He looked comfortable. His head was resting against the doorframe with his legs stretched out in front of him, one ankle crossed over the other.

She didn't have to ask him what he was doing. She already knew, and, dear God, how could she not love him? He was staying up all night just to make certain she was safe.

"Travis, I have a bolt on my door. You don't have to worry about me."

"Go back to bed."

"Will you please turn around and look at me? I'm trying to explain that—"

He didn't let her finish. "Are you in your nightgown?"

The question gave her pause. "Yes."

"You won't be wearing it for long if I turn around. Do you want me to be more specific?"

"No. Good night, Travis."

"I thought you'd see it my way."

She shut the door and leaned against it as the tears began to well up in her eyes. She couldn't cry, she told herself. She'd make too much noise, and then he'd know or at least suspect the awful truth.

She was in love with him.

Emily didn't get much sleep that night, yet she felt refreshed when she came downstairs the following morning. She had made several momentous decisions about her future during the black hours of the night, and for the first time in a long while, she felt as though she were in control again. Ever since the fiasco with

Randolph, she'd jumped into one rash thing after another, but fortunately she had finally come to her senses.

She was relieved because she'd realized in time the terrible mistake she would have made if she married Mr. O'Toole. She was also heartsick, because she knew she was going to have to leave Travis.

He was never going to know how she really felt about him. He wasn't the marrying kind, and if she told him she loved him, she would only make him feel uncomfortable. He might also feel sorry for her, and that possibility horrified her.

Come hell or high water, she was going to be cheerful around him. She could cry as much as she wanted once she was on the stagecoach and headed for home. Travis, however, wasn't going to see a single tear.

"Isn't it a fine day, Millie?" she called out as she walked into the kitchen. "Good morning, Travis," she added when she saw him coming in the back door.

He scowled back at her and mumbled something that might have been a greeting. He was obviously in a foul mood, and she decided to pretend she didn't notice.

Millie placed a large bowl of oatmeal on the table for her. Emily sprinkled it with sugar and ate every bit of it. She drank two full glasses of milk too.

Millie wasn't in a very good mood either. Her gaze darted back and forth between Emily and Travis, and every now and then, she'd mutter something to herself and shake her head.

The second Travis left to saddle their horses, she sat down beside Emily.

"Are you still hell-bent on going to Golden Crest?"

Millie's colorful use of words made Emily smile. "Yes," she answered. "But I—"

"For the love of the Almighty, stop being so stubborn. You're in for a life of heartache if you marry the wrong man."

Emily reached over and patted her hand. She found Millie's outrage and concern endearing. "I'm not going to marry Clifford O'Toole."

Millie's head snapped up. "You're not?"

"No, I'm not, but I owe it to him to tell him so face-to-face."

"Hogwash."

"It's the right thing to do," Emily insisted.

"Does Travis know about this?"

She shook her head. "I'll tell him later, when he's in a better mood. Besides, if I tell him now, he might not take me to Golden Crest, and I really owe it to Mr. O'Toole to explain my reasons for changing my mind."

John came into the kitchen with her satchels in his arms. "I'll just give these to Travis," he remarked as he hurried out the back door.

Emily spotted Travis leading the horses out of the barn. She stood up and turned to Millie.

"Thank you for worrying about me."

"That's what friends do for one another, don't they?"

Emily became teary-eyed. "Yes," she agreed.

"Will you stop by on your way back?"

"I'll try," she promised.

Millie patted her on her shoulder. "You've got a good heart, girl. Don't let anyone tell you different."

Emily felt as if she were leaving her best friend. She hurried out the door before she started crying, stopped long enough to thank John, and then ran to Travis.

The couple stood side by side as they watched Emily and Travis leave.

They'd been riding for almost an hour before Emily broke the silence to ask Travis a question. "How long will it take to get to Golden Crest?"

"A while," he answered. "Are you in a hurry?"

"Yes," she began. She was going to tell him that the sooner they got to their destination, the sooner they could leave, but Travis's blasphemy distracted her.

"Hell."

"I beg your pardon?"

"Hell," he muttered once again.

His mood obviously hadn't improved. She waited several minutes before speaking to him again. "I'd like to ask a favor of you."

"No."

She ignored his reply. "When we get to Golden Crest, I would appreciate it if you wouldn't contradict me. No matter what I say to Mr. O'Toole, please go along with it. All right?"

"You're going to pull your helpless act again, aren't you? If he isn't a complete idiot, and I have my doubts about that, he'll see right through your little charade."

She let out a loud sigh in frustration. "Will you try to get along? And don't you dare call me crazy again," she added when he turned in his saddle to give her a hard, you're-out-of-your-mind look.

"If the petticoat fits, Emily . . ."

"Oh, and please don't call me Emily in front of him."

"The petticoat fits all right."

She refused to argue. She thought about telling him what her plan was, then decided that because he was in such a horrible mood, he would just have to wait to find out. Besides, in his present frame of mind, she was pretty certain that if she admitted she was going to tell Mr. O'Toole the wedding was off, Travis would turn the horses around and head back to Pritchard. He wouldn't understand how important it was for her to explain in person instead of sending a note. She could never be so cruel to anyone. She knew firsthand how it felt.

Emily spent the rest of the journey worrying. She hoped Mr. O'Toole didn't have a temper, for the thought of having an out-and-out confrontation with him made her stomach ache, and by the time they started the climb up the last hill to the crest, she was so nervous, her hands were visibly shaking.

When they rounded the curve, Travis saw the shotgun trained on the two of them through the branches in the trees.

She saw the dilapidated shack leaning precariously to one side in the center of the dirt yard at the very top of the crest and frowned in reaction. Where was Mr. O'Toole's grand house? He had told her in his letters that his home was nestled in the clouds at the very tip, and since she and Travis couldn't possibly climb any higher without falling off the mountain, she could only come to one conclusion. Travis had obviously taken a wrong turn and Mr. O'Toole's fine house was on the other side of the crest.

"Emily, move closer to my right side. Do it now."

The tone of his whisper didn't suggest she dally. She nudged her horse forward into the narrow opening between the rock ledge and Travis, but she didn't really become alarmed until she glanced over and saw his dark expression.

"Is something wrong?" she whispered back.

"Maybe."

He was staring intently at a clump of trees to the west. Something fascinated him, all right. Emily leaned forward in her saddle, peeked around him, and gave the area a thorough once-over. She still couldn't see anything amiss and decided then that he was just being overly cautious.

She turned back to the shack just as the front door opened with a loud groan and a ridiculously attired man came hurrying outside. Her eyes widened, for, honest to Pete, she'd never seen anyone like him. He was tall, skinny, and so filthy he could have blended into the dirt if he hadn't been wearing a ludicrous formal black top hat and red satin suspenders over a stained undershirt and brown pants.

She watched him adjust the straps as he moved toward her. "Good Lord," she whispered.

Travis waited until the man had reached the center of the yard before ordering him to stop. "Tell your friend to drop his shotgun or I'll shoot him."

The stranger didn't like being told what to do. He squinted his eyes into slits and stared at Travis a long minute before he gave in.

"Git on out of them trees, Roscoe," he shouted before turning his attention to Emily.

"Are you the Finnegan woman?" he demanded.

Travis didn't give her time to answer. "Who are you?"

His gaze darted back and forth between the two of

them. Emily thought he was trying to decide if he should lie or tell the truth. The disgusting man reminded her of a rodent, and every time he glanced her way, she could feel her stomach tighten.

"O'Toole. Clifford O'Toole. Is she our bride?"

Emily let out a gasp. Dear God, the rodent and Clifford O'Toole were one and the same.

"No, I'm not your bride," she blurted out.

"Our bride?" Travis asked at the very same time.

"We're sharing her," Clifford explained in a matter-of-fact voice. "Like brothers do," he added with a shrug, and Emily could have sworn she saw a bug fly out from under his hat.

"How many brothers?" Travis asked in the same mild tone of voice that Clifford had used.

"Just Roscoe and me," he answered before his gaze settled on Emily once again. "You're her, ain't you?"

She frantically shook her head. "No," she insisted.

It wasn't the answer he was looking for, she realized. His hand moved toward the gun tucked in his waistband. Clifford gave Travis a quick glance, then suddenly changed his mind. His hand dropped back to his side.

"Then who are you?"

She straightened her shoulders, gave him a scathing look, and said, "I'm Mrs. Travis Clayborne."

If Travis was surprised by her lie, he didn't show it. His attention remained on the brother, Roscoe, who was now running toward Clifford.

Emily was too shaken to look at him. The meaning behind Clifford's explanation had finally sunk in. The two brothers intended to share the same woman, and, dear God, just thinking about it made her want to throw up. She continued to stare at the loathsome rodent in front of her, and, oh, how she wanted to lash out at him for lying to her in his letters.

She shook her head. No, he couldn't have written them, she realized. The letters were written by a refined gentleman, and it was apparent that there wasn't a refined bone in Clifford's body. He couldn't have written poetry either, of course, and she sincerely doubted he could even read or write his own name.

What in God's name had she gotten them into?

She made the mistake of looking at Roscoe then. He resembled his brother and was certainly just as filthy. His hair wasn't covered with a formal top hat though. He had a red silk scarf wrapped around it like a turban, and from the way he was grinning up at her, she thought he believed he was quite fashionable.

Emily wanted to leave with all possible haste. She found Roscoe vile and disgusting, but Clifford was worse. He frightened her. There was a mean look in his eyes that made her skin crawl.

Travis also wanted to leave, but at the moment he had his hands full. He knew there had to be at least one more man stalking them, and he was trying to find him and keep his attention on Clifford and Roscoe at the same time.

"If you ain't ours, what are you doing here?" Clifford asked.

"We took a wrong turn," she lied. "Travis, we should leave now."

"Don't go rushing off nowhere," Clifford insisted.

"If she ain't our woman, then where is she?" Roscoe asked his brother.

"You seen a woman going by the name of Finnegan?" Clifford asked her.

She was going to tell them no, then changed her mind. If they thought their bride was on her way to them, they might be more willing to let her and Travis leave in peace.

From the looks on the brothers' faces, she knew it was a remote possibility, but it was all she had and she latched onto it with a vengeance.

"As a matter of fact, my husband and I did meet a lady named Finnegan. Now, what did she tell me to call her? Barbara? No, that wasn't it. Emily," she added with a nod.

"Is she perty?" Roscoe asked.

"Oh, yes, she's very pretty."

"Where'd you meet up with her?" Clifford asked.

"We were just leaving the Perkinses' home when she arrived. Her escort will probably bring her to you tomorrow."

"Just one man riding shotgun with her?" Clifford wanted to know.

Emily nodded. "Yes. I recall his name too. Daniel Ryan. Perhaps you've heard of him."

The brothers shook their heads. "We don't recollect him," Roscoe told her. "Why'd you suppose we would?"

"Because he has quite a reputation," Emily said. She was grimacing inside over the tremor in her voice and prayed they couldn't hear it. If they knew how afraid she was, they might jump to the conclusion that she was lying, and then her game would be over.

"He's a United States marshal."

Clifford scowled. Roscoe spit on the ground. "A

lawman coming up here?" Roscoe muttered to his brother. "I don't like the sound of that."

"I don't like it neither," Clifford said.

Travis wasn't paying much attention to the conversation. His gaze continued to scan the trees, looking for the enemy.

"Maybe we can get us two brides," Roscoe whispered loud enough for both Emily and Travis to hear.

Clifford nodded, and it was apparent from the way he was staring at Travis that he'd already made up his mind.

Travis saw the silver gleam coming from the tree to the east just as Clifford let out a shout.

"Shoot him down, Giddy."

Travis's gun was out of his holster and firing before Clifford had finished bellowing the obscene order. A scream came from the trees, a branch snapped, and everyone but Travis turned to watch the brothers' cohort crash to the ground.

Clifford and Roscoe were smart enough not to go for their weapons. Roscoe dropped the shotgun and put his hands in the air, but Clifford stubbornly kept his hands down at his sides. They were balled into fists.

"He killed Giddy," Roscoe muttered.

"There weren't no call for that," Clifford said.

The two brothers shared a nod and then began to slowly edge apart.

They stopped when Travis cocked his gun.

"Take the lead down the hill," Travis told Emily.

He didn't have to repeat himself. She was so terrified now she almost dropped the reins when she forced her mount to back up and turn around.

Travis hadn't spared her a single glance from the

moment he'd spotted the bastard hiding in the trees with his shotgun. He ignored her now while he continued to search for more brothers lurking about, waiting for an opportunity to ambush him, but, damn, he couldn't find them, and time was running out.

He made Roscoe and Clifford remove their guns and toss them in the water trough and then made them do the same thing with their boots. Once they were finished, he ordered them to lie on their stomachs with their hands up over their heads.

He still didn't take his gaze off them, trusting his horse to find his way down the path while he turned in his saddle so he could keep his gun trained on them.

He didn't turn around until the brothers were out of sight, and when he did, he goaded his stallion into a full gallop. He reached Emily's side, slapped her mount on his hindquarters, and sent him flying into a gallop too.

He deliberately stayed behind her so that he could protect her back, and for that reason, he was an easy target. The shot still caught him by surprise. The bullet went into his back, and damn, but it burned. He could feel himself slipping to the side, and with his last ounce of strength, he threw himself forward. He grabbed hold of his horse's mane with his left hand and tried to turn so he could fire his gun with his other hand.

He was too weak to lift his weapon. Emily was stopping now to help him. He tried to tell her to keep going, but all he could get out was one harsh word.

"No."

And then she was by his side and taking his gun away from him. He tried to focus on her, but the blackness before his eyes was making it impossible. He knew it would only be a matter of seconds before he passed out, and he desperately wanted to get her to safety first.

"Get out of here," he whispered.

"Hold on," Emily cried out.

She reached over, took the reins away from him, and forced his stallion to veer with hers toward the cluster of trees near the base of the first incline. Shots echoed around them as they entered the protection of the pines. The horses made another sharp turn before coming to an abrupt stop at the edge of a bluff.

Travis tried to sit up, but realized his mistake when he felt himself falling. He heard Emily scream his name a scant second before the darkness claimed him.

She swung her leg over her horse and leapt to the ground. "Get up, Travis," she begged as she ran to him. "Please, God, don't let him be dead."

He'd landed on his side and was half draped over a boulder. His head had struck the rock, and there were splatters of blood everywhere.

She knelt down beside him and gently turned him so she could see his back. She screamed then, a piercing, agonizing scream, and something seemed to explode inside her. She was filled with such rage she could barely think.

A shot stung the rock beside him. Emily came to her senses in the blink of an eye. She put Travis's gun back in his holster so she could use both her hands, put her arms under his, and began to drag him to safety.

She thought only to get him further into the forest. Then she saw a deep crevice between the rocks at one end of the bluff and turned around to drag him there. No one could get to him from behind, she knew, and they couldn't attack from the sides either. They would have to come at them head-on, and then she would shoot them down like the rabid dogs they were.

She didn't know where her strength came from, but she thought that maybe God was lending her a hand now. She tucked Travis into the crevice, rolled him on his side, and then took his gun in her hands again.

Roscoe came at them first. She shot him in the thigh. He yelped in fury and hopped back out of sight.

"The bitch got me, Clifford," he roared. "I got to kill her now."

"You hit bad?" Clifford shouted back.

"I'm bleeding like a pig, but it's just a flesh nick. I'm gonna kill her, all right."

"Not till we take a turn using her," Clifford shouted. "We'll hurt her good, Roscoe."

The two brothers continued to shout at one another. They were trying to terrify her, as each described in vile detail what he was going to do to her. She was already scared out of her wits, however, and nothing they could say now would make it any worse.

As long as the shouts remained distant, she knew she and Travis were safe. She put his gun down on the ground next to her, lifted her skirt, and ripped her petticoat so she could fashion a bandage for him. There was blood on the front of Travis's shirt on the left side. She tore his shirt free, saw the small hole in his skin, and realized the bullet had gone straight through. His back was covered in blood. She pressed the cloth to the injury and used another long strip of her petticoat to wrap around him.

The shouting suddenly stopped. Emily grabbed the

gun and waited. A second felt like an hour. Roscoe poked his head out through the branches of a tree. He moved back before she could aim.

"She's tucked in tight between the rocks," he shouted to his brother. "The only way we can get to her is head-on. She'll kill us then."

"Don't you worry none. We'll get her," Clifford called back.

She didn't believe she could become more terrified. Then Rosco shouted to his brother. "We going to starve her out of them rocks?"

"No, we'll rush her during the night. She won't see us coming at her in the dark."

She began to pray again. She knew their chances of surviving were almost nonexistent, but if God could please send them some help, she would be most appreciative. If He wanted one of them to die, then please let it be her. All of this was her fault, not Travis's, and he was just a good, decent man. He didn't deserve to die this way.

God didn't answer her prayer for what seemed like hours, and during that time she was taunted by the hoots and shouts of Clifford and Roscoe.

He did answer her though, and she realized then she should have been a little more specific with her request.

He sent her One-Eyed Jack.

"Miss Emily, are you all right?"

She heard the whisper coming from below the bluff.

"Who is it?" she whispered back.

No one answered until she repeated her question a second time.

"It's me—Jack."

"Jack? Is that really you?"

"I just said it was."

"Are you below Travis and me on the rocks?"

"I skittered out on a ledge. Don't worry; no one can get any higher without pitching off into the canyon."

"Jack, the O'Toole brothers are trying to kill us."

"I figured as much as soon as I heard the gunshots. I can't get to you, Miss Emily."

"Could you please go and get help? Travis was shot in the back."

"He's a goner then," Jack whispered.

"No," she screamed in denial.

"No call to shout at me."

She heard the stubborn edge in his voice and knew he was getting his back up. God, she didn't have time for this. Didn't Jack realize how dangerous their situation was?

"I'm sorry," she whispered. "Oh, Jack, I'm so scared. Thank you for following us."

"I didn't do it for him. I did it for you. I'm taken with you, Miss Emily, and I've come to declare my intentions."

"Jack, now isn't the time," she cried out. "Please go and get help for us."

"It'll cost you. I'm wanting the five dollars back and five more so I can buy me some fancy courtin' clothes. Don't go getting the notion I'm wanting to marry you though. I got something else in mind."

She squeezed her eyes shut. She didn't want him to waste time talking, but she knew Jack well enough to understand he couldn't be pushed. He would leave to get help when he was ready and not a second before.

"Don't you want to know what I'm wanting?"

"Yes, Jack, tell me what you want." She sounded frantic. She couldn't help it.

"I'm wanting you to have supper with me down at the dining room in the Pritchard hotel. You got to latch onto my arm and let me walk you in too, and you can't get up and leave 'fore I do. Is it a deal?"

"Yes, it's a deal."

"I'll be leaving then."

"Hurry, Jack, and be careful."

Travis groaned then, but Emily couldn't take her attention away from the entrance to their hideaway long enough to see if his eyes were open or closed.

"It's going to be all right, Travis," she whispered.

Clifford came flying across the entrance. She didn't even have time to cock her gun before he reached the other side. She had to put both hands on Travis's gun to keep it steady. Her arms were outstretched in front of her. Tears streamed down her face, but she didn't dare take her hand away from the gun to wipe them away. She needed to concentrate, and most of all, she needed to pray.

Travis opened his eyes and looked at her. He saw the gun in her hands, heard her sob low in her throat, and wanted more than anything to take her into his arms and comfort her. He couldn't move. He knew something was wrong, yet he couldn't figure out what it was. He thought he must be pinned against something, and whatever it was was burning the hell out of his back.

He tried to focus on his surroundings. Emily was sitting in front of him with her back pressed up against his chest. There were two long lines side by side in the dirt leading up to her, and he had to think about it for a long while before he realized someone had dragged something heavy across the narrow clearing.

She'd dragged him to safety. Dear God, it all came back with startling clarity then. He'd been shot, and Emily was sitting in front of him to protect him. The O'Toole brothers must still be out there, and he'd left Emily to fend for both of them.

She needed to get the hell out of there.

He whispered her name and willed himself to stay awake. "Emily, what are you doing? You've got to leave."

She didn't turn around when she answered him. "It's all right, my love," she whispered. "You can sleep now. I'll keep you safe."

Who was keeping her safe? No, no, it was wrong. He should protect her, he knew, and, Lord, he didn't want to sleep; he wanted to take the gun out of her hands and shoot the bastards because they'd made her cry. Then the black waves were suddenly rushing toward him, and he was once again pulled under into the dark.

She didn't know how long she sat there, hoping and praying. Their situation was becoming hopeless. Dusk was fast approaching, and she doubted help would arrive before nightfall. She reminded God that hopeless situations weren't difficult for Him, and though she didn't know what would happen, she was fully prepared for the worst. Only one thought drove her now. She would die protecting the man she loved.

Nine

The sound of gunfire at close range jarred Travis awake. It took him a long while to find the strength to open his eyes, and when at last he succeeded, he thought he was looking up at the blue sky.

Suddenly the sky began to move. He couldn't understand what was happening. He closed his eyes and tried to concentrate on the whispers floating around him, and when he was able to focus again, he saw a man leaning over him . . . a big man, with blue eyes. Was it Cole? No, he realized, it wasn't his brother. It was someone else.

The stranger was moving him. Travis's head dropped down to his chest, but his eyes remained open. He stared in puzzlement at a gleaming gold object the stranger wore clipped to his leather vest. He thought it was a pocket watch.

He heard Emily whisper. She asked the stranger if there was still time to get to the Perkinses' home before dark, and it was only when she called the man "Mr. Ryan" that everything clicked into place. His gaze moved from the gold case up to the blue eyes, then back again.

No, it wasn't a pocket watch as he'd assumed. It was a compass.

The bastard pulling him every which way was wearing Cole's compass. Travis became incensed. He let out a low growl and tried to rip his brother's gift away from the stranger, but, damn, he was so weak, he couldn't even lift his hand.

The effort drained his strength. He felt as though someone had put a hand on top of his head and was shoving him under the water again.

And then he slept.

Travis came awake with a start to find Millie Perkins leaning over him with a razor in her hands. Instinctively, he knocked the razor out of her grasp and sent it flying across the room. It landed on the dresser, skated across, and dropped to the floor.

He'd given Millie quite a start. She jumped back and let out a shout. "Lord, you're quick. I see you've finally decided to come back to us."

"How long have I been asleep?"

"Off and on, almost four days now. You needed sleep to get your strength back, at least that's what the doctor told us. He must have been right because the glazed look is gone from your eyes now. I was going to shave you," she added with a nod. "You could sure use it. You're starting to resemble a bear."

Travis rubbed his whiskered jaw. "I'll do it," he said. He yawned, stretched the muscles in his shoulders, and felt only a twinge of fire. "I was shot."

"Yes, you most certainly were," she agreed. "They got you in the back, but more to your side than in the center. The bullet went on through, and the doctor assured us there isn't any chance of an infection now because you didn't catch a fever. You were sure lucky. You had an angel looking out for you."

Travis smiled. "I must have," he agreed. His gaze slowly moved around the room. It was familiar to him, and it took him a minute or two to realize why. He was in the same bed Emily had slept in.

One thought jumped to another. "Where is she?"

Millie seemed hesitant to tell him. "I assume you're asking me about Emily. Do you remember any of the last four days? No, I don't suppose you do," she continued before he could answer. "Emily sat by your bed day and night, worrying and praying about you. Yesterday your sleep turned real peaceful, and when Doc Stanley came back by, he convinced her that the worst was over and that you would be just fine."

"Where is she?" he asked again. He could tell something was wrong from the way she was nervously smoothing down her apron and looking everywhere but at him. He had a feeling he wasn't going to like her answer.

She took a step back before answering. "She's gone."

He immediately threw off the covers and swung his legs over the side of the bed. Millie's hands flew to her eyes, and she turned around so quickly she almost lost her balance. He realized then he didn't have any clothes on, let out a whispered expletive, and dragged the covers back up. He leaned against the headboard and muttered, "Damn, I'm weak."

"You should be weak. You lost some blood, but not too much, according to Doc Stanley. It was the hit you took to your head when you fell off your horse and struck a rock that made you sleep so long."

"I fell off my horse?" He was horrified by the mere thought. Cole would have a heyday with that bit of news if he ever found out. His brother would never let him live it down.

"Millie, you can turn around now."

She was blushing like an old spinster and still smoothing her apron when she did as he suggested.

"According to Emily, you did fall off your horse. She was the angel looking out for you, Travis. She dragged you a good long way to safety, and if you don't mind me saying so, that woman loves you more than any other woman ever will, and you're a fool if you don't go after her."

Travis shook his head. "She was all set to marry O'Toole, remember? And do you know why? Because she was hell-bent on marrying a rich man with a grand house and a curved damned staircase."

The longer he thought about it, the madder he became. What kind of a woman would take off without even bothering to say good-bye first? A damned inconsiderate one, that's who.

Millie, he noticed, was vehemently shaking her head at him. "She was not going to marry O'Toole. She told me so before you took her up to the crest."

"No, she decided against marrying him the second she saw him and his shack."

Millie snorted. "You sure are getting yourself worked up into a lather about it. If I were you, I'd get out of that bed and go after her before it's too late."

"I ought to, just to give her a piece of my mind. It was downright thoughtless of her to sneak out like that. Did she leave in the dead of night?"

"No, of course she didn't. She left in the light of day. She's on her way home to Boston, as a matter of fact. I was telling John that sooner or later, some other man is going to snatch her up. Oh, Emily's made up her mind never to marry because of what happened, but in time some smooth-talking man will be able to convince her. Of course, you won't care about her having another man's children, now will you?"

Travis refused to answer the question. "Why didn't she tell me she'd changed her mind before I took her up there?"

"Because she knew you wouldn't take her, that's why. She was determined to do the right thing and tell that no-good rodent face-to-face that she'd changed her mind."

"Rodent?"

"That's what she called him, all right. Of course, she didn't know he was a rodent before she met him. She believed he was a decent man and that she owed him an explanation."

"Let me get this straight. She thought she owed that bastard, but she couldn't wait around long enough for me to wake up?"

"She admitted it was her own foolish pride that landed her in this pickle and that she had learned a valuable lesson. She didn't tell me why she was leaving though. She knew the stagecoach only goes through Pritchard on Sunday, but she needed to go sooner. Guess you're going to have to go after her and ask her your questions. I can't answer them."

"I'm going back to Golden Crest and shoot those bastard brothers before I do anything else."

"The O'Tooles are already dead. A real nice gentleman shot them for you. It was a fair fight, I suppose, what with them trying to kill Emily and you. And the law's on his side," she added with a chuckle. "No doubt about that."

He didn't understand why she was so amused. "I guess I should thank him. Is he still here?"

She shook her head. "He took off right after he dropped you in that bed, but he stopped by yesterday on his way to Pritchard. Emily asked him if she could ride with him."

"You let her ride off with a stranger?"

"He didn't seem like a stranger to us, Travis. John talked to him a good long while. John was downstairs having an early snort with old man Kiley when they left. My husband was going to take Emily, but he was convinced he should stay here and look out for me. There's a gang hiding in these hills. You remember John telling you about them? They've done a lot of killing and robbing. They even murdered a young mother and her little girl."

Travis closed his eyes. "The man was Daniel Ryan, wasn't he?"

"Yes."

He remembered everything . . . those cold, piercing blue eyes . . . and the gleaming gold compass. . . .

"He was wearing my brother's compass."

"He sure was," she agreed. "Emily asked him to give it to her, but he wouldn't. He let her hold the gold case and showed her how to open the little clasp so she could take the compass out and get a good look at it. Then he made her give it back to him. He told her he had to return it to the lady it belonged to, and Emily understood. Now, Travis, don't look at me like that. That lawman saved your life and Emily's too, because she never would have seen the O'Tooles sneaking up on the two of you in the dark. They would have nabbed her for sure, and you know what would have happened then. Ryan got there in the nick of time."

The thought of Emily being in such danger scared the hell out of him. It also infuriated him. If she had only taken the time to tell him what she planned to do, he never would have taken her up there in the first place and she wouldn't have ended up in such a godawful position.

"That woman doesn't have the sense God gave her."

"I guess it's up to you to find her some, then."

He ignored her remark. "Hell, I can't shoot Ryan."

Millie opened the door before commenting on his outrageous remark. "Of course you can't kill him. Will it make you feel any better to know that Emily shot at him? She thought he was one of the O'Tooles. Ryan told me he sure was surprised."

"I'm not surprised. She shoots at every man she meets," he exaggerated.

Millie let out a loud sigh. "You're a stubborn man, Travis Clayborne. Are you going to go down to Pritchard or not?"

He didn't like being prodded one bit. "I'm buck naked and on my way to shut the door, Millie."

She let out a screech and went running down the hallway. He slammed the door behind her.

Travis was in a foul mood by the time he finished washing and dressing. He cut himself shaving because he wasn't paying any attention to what he was doing. He was too busy thinking about Emily.

He made up his mind on his way down to the kitchen. By God, he was going to go to Pritchard so he could tell the ungrateful woman exactly how he felt. He would get a proper good-bye out of her too.

And that was all he was willing to admit.

Ten

They were the talk of the town. People started gathering in the middle of the afternoon, and within an hour, the Pritchard hotel was packed to capacity. The overflow spilled out into the street, and more lined the walkway on the other side.

Traffic came to a standstill, shops closed early, and chores were all but forgotten. This was a momentous occasion, after all, and no one wanted to miss it.

The clock inside the lobby began to chime the hour, and at six o'clock on the dot on Saturday evening, One-Eyed Jack Hanrahan came sashaying into the hotel, looking just about as fine as a man could look.

Money started changing hands immediately. Some of the men in town had bet Jack wouldn't show up; others had been just as certain he would. Olsen, the proprietor of the establishment, didn't believe in gambling, but he still managed to make a small fortune for himself and his staff because he'd been clever enough to charge admission to enter the dining room. He had fancy placement cards made too, and anyone who wanted to sit close to Jack Hanrahan and Emily Finnegan while they dined had to pay dearly for the privilege. In the event Miss Finnegan didn't keep her promise—and what woman in her right mind would?—the proprietor had a sign propped up on the counter to alert everyone that there wouldn't be any talk about refunds.

Olsen didn't feel at all guilty about fleecing his friends and neighbors, for one simple but important reason: history was in the making that day, and all because Jack had finally taken a bath.

Folks had bet on that too, so there was a fair amount of grumbling from the losers when the shout came echoing down the street at precisely five o'clock that Jack Hanrahan had just been seen entering the bathhouse.

The sight of the mountain man, now all squeaky clean and gussied up, was enough to take the crowd's breath away and was surely worth every penny they'd paid. Why, Jack looked as pretty as you please dressed in a starched white shirt, pale blue tie without a stain anywhere, and black twill trousers with a nice straight crease down each pant leg, exactly where it was supposed to be. His shoes were new and shiny; his hair was all slicked down, and he carried a black suit jacket over his arm, just like a dapper gentleman would on a warm day.

The crowd began to cheer as they watched Jack make quite a production of putting his coat on and adjusting his brand-new eye patch, but one mean look from him was all it took to slam the door shut on that nonsense.

The man had a flair, all right. He also had a temper as big as the territory. Olsen nervously waited behind the counter next to his "No Refunds" sign while Jack easily threaded his way through the crowd. He would have gotten to the proprietor sooner, but he paused twice to glare at offenders in the crowd who dared to get too close to him. Folks were squeezed up so tight against one another, they could barely breathe let alone move, yet like the Red Sea, they miraculously parted to give him room. No one dared touch him because that just might make him mad, and only God knew what he would do then.

Olsen was shaking from head to toe. He didn't want to be around when Jack found out Miss Finnegan had changed her mind—if indeed she had—and so he made one of the servants go upstairs with him to announce her escort's arrival. Olsen didn't plan on coming back down. He'd send the servant with the bad news while he sought out a safe hiding place.

With the thought of survival uppermost in his mind, he motioned to a staff member, told Jack in a stammer he would be pleased to go and fetch Miss Finnegan, and then hurried around the counter.

The boy he'd recently hired met him at the bottom of the staircase, and just as the two of them were about to start up, they spotted Miss Emily at the landing.

Money would have changed hands again if the men could have stopped gawking at the beautiful woman long enough to get the bills out of their pockets. Because of the size of the crowd, the noise should have been deafening. It wasn't though. In fact, no one made a sound. They all stared in wonder, astonishment . . . and relief at the lovely lady above them.

She was stunning. Dressed for a formal ball, she wore a full-length shimmering gold gown with a modestly revealing neckline meant to entice men and placate women, capped sleeves, and a fitted bodice that showed off her figure to perfection. The skirt was full and fell in soft folds around her golden slippers, and when she moved toward the top step, the fabric sparkled and glittered in the candlelight.

Travis watched her from the entrance to the alcove behind the counter. While the crowd would probably never forget what she wore, he was far more enamored by the warmth that came into her eyes when she found Jack in the sea of faces below her and smiled at him.

Travis moved back into the dark before she turned toward him. He was there only to make certain there wasn't any trouble, and unless it was absolutely necessary, he wasn't going to interfere. The evening belonged to Jack Hanrahan, but tomorrow belonged to him.

He shook his head in amazement when Jack moved to the bottom of the steps and put his hand out to her. The gesture was gallant, and obviously pleased Emily, for her smile widened and her eyes began to sparkle.

Travis was suddenly having difficulty catching his breath. The closer she got to him, the faster his heart beat until it was thundering in his ears. The heat was getting to him, he told himself, and surely that was the reason he was feeling so peculiar. He loosened the collar of his shirt. Odd, but that didn't help at all.

Emily was as regal as a princess as she came down the stairs. Her head was held high and her attention was centered on her escort and no other. She reached Jack's side, placed her hand on his arm, and walked close to him into the dining room.

The crowd was all but climbing the walls to give them enough room.

For the hardworking people in Pritchard, it just kept getting better and better after that. It was indeed a magical night for everyone, for not only did Jack eat with utensils, he also patiently waited after supper for the servants to remove the tables from the center of the room so he and Emily could dance.

They were the only couple on the floor. Jack stunned everyone once again when he took Emily into his arms. The couple glided around the room to the gyrating sounds of Billie Bob and Joe Boy's Band. Jack proved to be light on his feet and, in fact, was far more graceful than any other man there. He oozed charm as well, and Miss Emily Finnegan, the crowd decided, was having the time of her life.

The evening ended at one o'clock in the morning when Joe Boy's arm wore out from sawing his fiddle. Jack escorted Emily to the lobby again. He clasped hold of her fingers, leaned down, and kissed her hand. He whispered something to her too that made her burst into laughter. Jack even managed a grin, and after she kissed his cheek, he actually smiled.

He waited until Emily had gone upstairs, then turned and strutted out of the lobby as content as a man can be. By the time he'd reached the street, the eye patch was on the ground behind him, the jacket was draped over a hitching post, and his tie was in the water trough.

And the Jack Hanrahan they all knew and feared was back again.

Emily had just gotten into bed and pulled the covers up when she heard the scrape of a chair or a crate being dragged along the hallway floor. She bolted upright, threw her covers off, and ran across the room to make certain the latch was properly secured.

She had remembered to turn the lock after all. She leaned against the door for several minutes. Blessedly, the sound wasn't repeated, and she decided then that whoever or whatever it was had gone away.

She returned to her bed and got down to the more important business at hand. She desperately needed to cry, and she fervently hoped that by the time she was finished, she would have gotten Travis out of her mind.

She didn't succeed; crying didn't help one bit.

It was time to go home.

Eleven

She had overslept. She was going to miss the stagecoach if she didn't hurry. There wasn't even time for breakfast, which was fine with her because she was too upset to eat anything anyway. She dressed as quickly as possible, threw her things into her satchels, and ran downstairs to ask one of the staff members to please take her bags to the station.

Her luggage got there a few minutes before she did. Fortunately the street was deserted, so she didn't have to worry about anyone trying to engage her in conversation. She simply wasn't in the mood to be civil today.

She wasn't in the mood to go back home either, but she was still going to do it. She tried to be happy about seeing her family again. She couldn't manage it though. Going back to Boston wasn't her only solution, but it was definitely the safest one, because she knew that if she stayed here, she'd throw herself at Travis in no time at all and become thoroughly ruined. And wouldn't her parents just love that.

Emily's patience was about worn out when the stagecoach came barreling around the corner on two wheels and pulled to a rocking stop in front of her. Dust flew up around her, and she hurriedly moved back behind her satchels to get away from it.

The driver was a tall, lanky man with a curt, no-nonsense way about him. He jumped down from his seat, adjusted his bright blue bandanna around his neck, and tipped the brim of his hat to her.

"I'm running late, ma'am. You'd best get on inside while I fill up my water jug. I'll tell you my rules when I come back out."

He opened the door for her before he went inside the station. A few minutes later, he came out again and began to throw her satchels up on the roof of the coach.

He spoke as rapidly as he worked. "If you hear any gunshots, you hit the floor. Try to curl up under one of the seats. Don't look out the window, no matter how much you want to. I just can't tell you how important that rule is, ma'am, so try to remember. I'm not expecting trouble, but I'm always ready for it. Now, if you're needing to stop for a minute, lean on out the window and shout at me. Unless you hear gunshots first. Then don't lean out. I'm hoping you won't need to stop though, because that will make me even later getting to my next town."

"I won't need to stop," she promised.

He climbed up on top of the coach, tied the satchels, then jumped down and opened the door again.

"You got your ticket ready?"

"Yes." She handed it to him and sat back against the warm leather bench.

He gave her a sharp look. "Is something wrong, ma'am? You got tears in your eyes. It's none of my business, of course, unless you're feeling puny. Then I ought to know about it."

"No, sir, I'm not sick. It's just the dust in the air that's making my eyes water."

"No need to call me sir. My name's Kelley. Now, if you do happen to get sick, well then, just lean on out the window and shout at me. Unless you hear gunshots. Then don't look out. I can't stress enough the importance of remembering that rule, ma'am."

He shut the door and climbed back up on his seat before she could even tell him what her name was much less assure him she wouldn't look out the window.

The coach gently rocked back when the horses turned and started down the main street. They gathered speed as they clipped along, and by the time they'd passed the general store near the center of the street, they were in a full gallop.

Emily folded her hands together in her lap and closed her eyes. The decision to leave had been made; there wasn't any going back, and she was determined to come to terms with the fact that she would never see Travis again. God willing, she might even find a little peace.

A gunshot suddenly rang out. Kelley let out a shout,

and Emily was flung forward when he pulled on the reins. The horses skidded to a stop.

Emily landed on the floor with her skirt draped over her head. She quickly got back up on her seat and adjusted her clothing. She saw people coming out of the hotel and couldn't help but notice that none of them looked very alarmed.

She couldn't imagine what was going on. She looked out the window to find out. Unfortunately, Kelley spotted her.

"Ah, now, I told you not to do that," he cried out.

"Mr. Kelley, what's happening?"

"Travis Clayborne's what's happening, ma'am."

She didn't even have time to react to Kelley's explanation before Travis's roar filled the carriage.

"Emily Finnegan, get out of that stagecoach. I want a word with you."

She was so startled by the command, she struck her head when she jumped back against the seat. She only stayed there a second or two. Then she leaned out the window again.

And that was when she saw Travis striding down the street toward her.

She was certain she was going to keel over from heart strain right then and there. He looked wonderful and sweet and adorable . . . and furious.

He walked with his usual arrogant swagger. The man was obviously feeling perky again, and when she considered how close he'd been to dying—at least she thought he'd been close, no matter what the doctor said—his recovery was almost miraculous.

She let out a sigh. As much as she dreaded it, she was going to have to tell him good-bye. She wouldn't cry, no matter how overwhelming the urge, and the sooner she got it said and done, the quicker she could leave.

She decided to meet him halfway. Yes, that was what she should do. She would shake his hand, tell him thank you and good-bye, and be on her way.

She had second thoughts as soon as she opened the door. She noticed the telltale, now-you're-going-to-get-it glint in his eyes, and promptly shut the door again. She thought she knew why he was there. He had gotten out of his sickbed and ridden all the way down to Pritchard from the Perkinses' home just to tell her she was crazy again. He was stubborn enough to do such a foolish thing.

"Mr. Kelley, make him go away."

"Begging your pardon, ma'am, but no one tells any of the Clayborne brothers what to do. You'd best get on out and find out what he wants."

Travis shouted to her again. "Now, Emily!"

She stepped out into the street, shut the door behind her, and started walking toward him.

"Don't you dare leave without me, Mr. Kelley."

"That's sort of up to Clayborne, ma'am."

She shook her head to let him know she didn't agree. She continued on toward Travis, muttering all the while. "If that man makes me cry, I swear I'm going to borrow his gun and shoot him. Just see if I don't."

Kelley heard her. "I'd be real surprised if Travis lets you have his gun, ma'am."

Emily ignored the driver. She stopped when she was about twenty feet away from Travis and put her hand out in a silent demand for him to stop where he was.

He ignored it.

"You were really going to do it, weren't you, Emily?"

"Do what?"

"Leave without saying good-bye."

"Travis, please lower your voice. You're drawing a crowd."

She turned to the boardwalk on her left and waved her hand at the group of men and women gathered there. "You there, move along, please. Go on, now."

When she noticed no one paid any attention to her request, she added a frown and then turned back to Travis.

"Yes, I was going to say good-bye."

"Is that so? Were you planning to shout it out the window of the stagecoach on your way out of town?"

"No, I wasn't going to shout it. I was going to write a letter to you."

His frown intensified. He didn't like hearing that bit of news at all. "You were going to write?"

She held her ground. For a second or two she thought Travis was going to keep on coming and walk right over her, but fortunately he stopped when he was a couple of feet away. She considered backing away from him, then changed her mind. He was deliberately trying to intimidate her, and she simply wasn't in the mood to put up with his antics today.

She was the one with the broken heart, for the love of God, and he had only gotten shot.

"Let me get this straight," he snapped. "You were hell-bent on going up to the crest so you could tell O'Toole face-to-face that you'd changed your mind and weren't going to marry him, but you didn't think you owed me the same consideration?"

"Millie told you."

"Damned right she told me," he said. "If you had mentioned your change of heart a little earlier . . ."

"You wouldn't have taken me up there."

"No, I wouldn't have. I wouldn't have gotten shot either, and you wouldn't have been in such a dangerous position. And by the way, Miss Finnegan, you won't be stepping out with any other men ever again, not even Jack Hanrahan. You got that?"

"Murder's frowned upon in these parts, Mr. Clayborne."

"Do you have any idea what would have happened to you if those bastards had gotten hold of you?"

"Yes," she cried out. "I know exactly what would have happened. I also know I almost got you killed. I'll never forgive myself for that. My only excuse is that I was trying to do the decent thing. If I'd known the O'Tooles were rodents, I assure you I wouldn't have gone up there. Oh, get it over with, why don't you? Tell me I'm crazy again. I know you want to."

"Fine. You're crazy. I swear you don't have a lick of sense in you."

"I'm not the one who got out of his sickbed and rode all the way to Pritchard just to tell someone she's crazy."

"That isn't why I came after you."

"Then why did you come here?"

She noticed he was having trouble coming up with an explanation. She also noticed the large crowd now surrounding the two of them. They seemed to have appeared out of thin air, and more were hurrying to join them.

She was appalled. "Don't you people have chores to do? This is a private conversation. Move away, now."

No one budged an inch. Out of the corner of her eye she saw a gentleman leaning against a hitching post. He had a wad of money in his hands, and each newcomer who arrived stopped to give him more before running into the street.

"Well, Travis? Why did you come after me?"

"I thought I wanted to give you a piece of my mind—" he began.

She interrupted him. "I wouldn't if I were you. You can't afford it. Now, if you don't mind, I'd like to get back inside the coach and be on my way. The driver has a schedule to keep. Mr. Kelley, where are you going?" she called out when she saw him running toward the man at the hitching post.

"Just making a friendly little bet, ma'am."

"Damn it, Emily, pay attention to me."

She was suddenly so miserable inside she wanted to scream. "Why should I? Everything is your fault. You made me fall in love with you, and now I'm so upset I can't think or sleep or eat."

She didn't realize what she'd blurted out until a woman behind her let out a little sigh. "She loves him."

Travis was looking outrageously complacent. She put her hand out toward him again to try to ward him off.

"I will recover from this affliction," she said. "Besides, loving you doesn't change a thing, so don't get any foolish notions. I'm going back to Boston."

"No, you're not."

"Yes, I am, and nothing you say to me will change my mind."

"You tell him, girl," a woman called out. "Don't let no man push you around."

"If she loves him, she ought to stay," someone else shouted.

The men in the crowd grunted their agreement. Emily was mortified by the audience. She turned to the woman who had suggested she stay, and whispered, "You don't understand. If I stay, I'll disgrace my parents and become thoroughly wanton."

The woman's head snapped up and her eyes widened. "Do you mean to say you would . . ."

Emily nodded. "That's exactly what I'm saying."

"You've got to go home, then," she stammered.

Travis threaded his fingers through his hair in frustration. The thought of losing Emily terrified him, and he didn't know how to make her stay.

God, she was stubborn.

"You love me, but you're leaving. Have I got that straight?"

"Yes," she answered. "I do love you, and I am leaving. It all makes perfectly good sense to me."

"Of course it does," he snapped.

She refused to argue with him. She turned around, waved for the crowd to get out of her way, and headed back to the stagecoach. She was almost running. Travis stayed right by her side.

The crowd chased after them.

"I vowed never to do another rash thing for the rest of my life, and staying here would not only be rash, it would also be sinful. I'm going home."

Travis was getting madder and madder by the second. He was consumed with panic and didn't like the feeling at all. He couldn't let her leave him. Didn't she understand how important she was to him? Without her, life wouldn't be worth living.

He didn't want to live without her.

The truth slapped him in the face, and he came to a dead stop. "Son of a gun," he whispered, "I love her."

Emily was sweet and good and loving, and all he wanted to think about now was keeping her by his side for the rest of his life. He was going to have to keep her out of that stagecoach first.

He caught up with her, heard her say something about a "rash" again, and patiently waited for her to finish rambling.

She finally stopped talking and gave him an expectant look. "Don't you agree?" she asked, wondering what had caused the sudden smile.

"Sure I do."

"She's leaving now," someone shouted from the back of the crowd.

"She'd be ruined if she stayed," a woman called out.

"Amen," someone else shouted.

They reached the stagecoach. Travis pulled the door open for her.

She put her hand out to him. "Good-bye, Travis."

"You expect me to shake your hand?"

"It would be the polite thing to do. Why are you smiling?"

"I'm a happy man."

She was crushed by the sudden change in his attitude. Her hand dropped back down to her side. "I'll write to you."

"That'll be nice."

"Will you write back?"

"Sure I will."

There wasn't anything left to say. She turned to get back inside the stagecoach then.

"Just one thing," he said.

"Yes?"

"Kiss me good-bye."

Twelve

She married a crazy man. She was so happy she couldn't stop smiling. She had even laughed out loud several times while she'd been in the bath, for she was filled with such an abundance of joy and love she couldn't keep it all inside.

She was waiting now for her husband to join her. She stood at the bedroom window above the Perkinses' parlor and stared out into the night while she brushed her hair. The moon was beautiful tonight, and the sky was alive with at least a hundred stars. Crickets were singing their nightly song in unison. The scent of pine filled the air, and everything seemed magical.

The long-stemmed pink rose Travis had given her

before the wedding ceremony was in a vase on the table beside her. She picked it up and held it against her heart.

She turned around when the door opened. Travis came inside, bolted the door, and turned to look at her. His breath caught in his throat, and he was suddenly overwhelmed by the beautiful woman he had managed to capture.

She was dressed in a prim white nightgown that covered her from the top of her neck to the bottom of her slippers.

"Good evening, Mrs. Clayborne."

She laughed, and he felt as though he'd just been embraced by her warmth. He leaned back against the door and grinned at her.

"Don't be nervous."

"Why do you think I'm nervous?"

"You just threw your brush out the window."

She laughed again. "I want it to be perfect for you."

"It already is."

It was the most perfectly wonderful thing he could have said to her. Oh, how she loved this man.

He removed his shirt, tossed it on the back of a chair, took off his shoes and socks next, and then came to her.

"You aren't really nervous, are you, sweetheart?"

"Just a little," she admitted. "I know what's going to happen. I'm just not familiar with the how."

"You mean you haven't made a thorough study on the subject?" he teased.

"No, but I imagine you have."

He took the rose out of her hand and slowly trailed

the fragrant bud down the side of her cheek. His gaze never left hers, and within seconds, the apprehension she had felt was gone.

"I love you, Emily. And only you," he told her in a rich, gruff voice.

Impatient to take her into his arms, he put the rose back in the vase and carried her over to the side of the bed. She kicked her slippers off on the way.

"Do you want me to explain in detail what I'm planning to do?"

She knew from the tone of his voice that he was teasing her. "No, thank you very much, but I appreciate the offer. I believe I'd rather you showed me."

He gently placed her in the center of the bed and came down on top of her, careful to brace his weight with his arms.

He leaned over her and stared into her eyes, savoring the love he saw there. "I'm going to make a thorough study of you, Mrs. Clayborne. God, I love the sound of that, and when I'm finished, it's my sincere hope you'll thank me very much."

He was tossing her favorite expressions back at her. The way he was looking at her, with such love and desire, filled her with anticipation, and if she had trusted her voice, she would have told him he didn't need to worry about putting her at ease now. She was more than ready to become his wife in the most intimate way. Heaven help her, she was eager.

Shivers raced down her spine when he nuzzled the side of her neck. She wrapped her arms around his shoulders and stroked his back.

He was determined to let her set the pace tonight,

and within minutes he was richly rewarded. She tugged on his hair, demanded he stop teasing her and give her a proper kiss. One was all it took for passion to explode between them. By the time he removed her gown and his trousers, she was breathless with excitement and he was having a hell of a time breathing at all.

He knew more about how her body would react to him than she did. His hands were strong yet incredibly gentle as he stroked the fire inside her.

And when at last they joined as one, it was all so astonishingly exquisite, she couldn't contain her cry. She was overwhelmed with the love she felt for this man. He made it so very perfect for her.

He felt her tighten around him, and he gave in to his own climax, shaking now because he had never experienced such splendor before.

It took a long while for either one of them to recover. They lay together in a tangle of legs and arms, and, damn, he was so happy and content he thought he must be in heaven.

She was so happy she needed to cry and laugh at the same time. The satisfied look on his face was comical to her. Then she realized she probably looked the same way.

He kept her in his arms when he rolled onto his back. She stretched out along his side and put her arm across his chest.

"Now, aren't you sorry you made me wait so long?"

She patted his chest while she gently corrected him. "It was only two weeks. You knew that stagecoach was going to leave while you were kissing me, didn't you?"

"Of course. Did you honestly think I would let you go?"

"I honestly think I'm happy you didn't."

He laughed. He was so pleased with her he had to kiss her again. Then he let his head drop back on the pillow and let out a loud, sleepy yawn.

"You put me through hell waiting to get my hands on you."

He was exaggerating, of course, at least she thought he was, and she wouldn't have given up the last two weeks for anything. He had proven to her during that time that he was possibly the most romantic man in the entire world. He'd courted her with what he referred to as a vengeance. She had never had a chance against him— he'd warned her about that—but she had held out for as long as possible to give him time to make certain he wanted to spend the rest of his life with her.

She had been concerned that it was only an infatuation on his part and therefore he saw only the good qualities in her. He had set her straight about her misconception at dinner the night before by cheerfully listing every single one of her flaws. It took him a long time to get them said too, and though she had been aware of a few, he pointed out several more she hadn't even known about. She was still stubbornly insisting that she wasn't stubborn at all.

"Do you know what I think, Travis? That one kiss good-bye led to this night."

He rolled her onto her back again. "I knew before then, and so did you. I love you."

"I love you too."

"Emily?"

"Yes?"

"Kiss me good-bye again."

Proof-of-Purchase

One Pink Rose

1319